W9-BRL-105

Poor People

Fyodor Dostoevsky

Translated by Hugh Aplin

ET REMOTISSIMA PROPE

100 PAGES

100 PAGES
Published by Hesperus Press Limited
4 Rickett Street, London SW6 1RU
www.hesperuspress.com

First published by Hesperus Press Limited, 2002

Introduction and English language translation © Hugh Aplin, 2002
Foreword © Charlotte Hobson, 2002

Designed and typeset by Fraser Muggeridge
Printed in the United Arab Emirates by Oriental Press

ISBN: 1-84391-023-3

CONTENTS

'Well, let me tell you, I don't believe that my fame will ever surpass the height it has now attained,' wrote Dostoevsky to his brother, Mikhail, in November 1845. *Poor People*, his first novel, was not to be published until the following January, but St Petersburg society was already abuzz with talk of this new literary talent. The first people to whom he showed his manuscript did not stop reading until they finished it at four in the morning, then rushed to find the author. Tears pouring down their cheeks, they embraced and congratulated him as 'the new Gogol'. The twenty-four-year-old author was speechless and embarrassed. It was not long before Vissarion Belinsky, the most influential literary critic of the day, had added his own commendation. Could Dostoevsky himself – Belinsky demanded – understand the tremendous significance of what he had written? No, he could not, he was too young and inexperienced. It was, Dostoevsky said, the most enchanting moment of his life, and it went straight to his head. 'Everyone considers me a phenomenon!' he boasted joyfully to his brother.

Belinsky's excitement was not simply pleasure at the discovery of a new voice. The liberal Russians of the 1840s, frustrated by their reactionary Tsar and longing for reform, placed all their hopes in literature. Belinsky insisted that the role of the author was to be a mouthpiece for a silenced population. 'Honour and glory to the young poet whose Muse loves those who live in garrets and basements, and speaks of them to the dwellers in gilded halls, saying, "See, these too are men and your brothers," he declaimed in his review of *Poor People*. Dostoevsky was to be the new protector of the 'Little Man', a conscience for the nation. This interpretation of the novel proved durable, providing the official line for Soviet critics, at least. But Dostoevsky himself almost certainly found it too simplistic. Only a few months after publication, Dostoevsky fell out with Belinsky, announcing that the latter understood nothing about literature.

'We all crawled out from under Gogol's *Greatcoat*,' Dostoevsky is supposed to have remarked. Whether apocryphal or not, it is a comment that applies particularly to *Poor People*, a grotesque version of the epistolary novel that was so popular in the early nineteenth century.

The protagonists are Makar Devushkin, a wretched, middle-aged copying-clerk in the civil service, and Varenka, a poor orphan in her late teens whose honour has been compromised in some unspecified but wicked way by the wealthy Mr Bykov. Much of the humour and poignancy arises from Devushkin's prose, which, with its folksy, colloquial and unintentionally revealing language, certainly owes a debt to Gogol. After a first, perfunctory reading, in fact, I was inclined to agree with the reviewers that claimed it was little more than an imitation of the great man.

Yet I was soon returning to pore over the text again, trying to make sense of its contradictions and ellipses. Even in this earliest work Dostoevsky's approach to the irrational is quite different from Gogol's. Where Gogol slides into the fantastic world of dreams and nightmares, Dostoevsky has already identified the area that he will spend his life investigating, and that, by the following century, will make him the most widely read Russian author in the world. *Poor People* soon emerges as a typically Dostoevskian study: an acute psychological portrait of a man driven to his limits.

And it is here, to my mind, that the excitement of Dostoevsky's first novel lies. He may not have formulated his extreme conservatism until much later in life, yet in *Poor People* the conflict between his liberal views and his acute awareness of human irrationality is already fierce. As in later books, he focuses above all on the irrationality of those who are struggling to survive. The very fact that a single illogical decision could push them over the edge into despair, that they have no safety net to allow them a little wavering, an eccentric action now and again, seems to draw people towards the brink. Devushkin and Varenka suffer from ill-health and the vulnerability of their position before rich and predatory men. But these conventional threats – the threats that a more didactic social commentator might be expected to dwell on – are made dramatically worse by their own, irresistible self-destructive urges. As Devushkin remarks, in what could be seen as the guiding principle of the tale: 'Poor men are capricious… that's the way nature arranges it.'

There is no doubt that Devushkin is a good man, self-sacrificing and generous. Yet, as we become adept at interpreting the contradictions and gaps in the letters, his selflessness starts to look more like fatal self-delusion. His longing to treat Varenka as a lady, to shower her with gifts and take her to the theatre almost drives both of them to starvation. His kindness is full of contradictions, and his flights of optimistic fancy are tainted by the admission the following evening that his 'head ached all day' – a hangover, we deduce. The man's slide into drunkenness is subtly developed, as the tone of the letters lurches from wild enthusiasm, to abject apology, to fatalism. Even his sympathy for those who are more desperate than himself is spoilt by the remark that 'To tell the truth, my dear, I began describing all this to you in part to get it off my chest, but more to show you an example of the good style of my writing…' His great ambition is to become a writer, someone whom passers-by point out on Nevsky Prospekt: 'Here comes the composer of literature and poet, Devushkin!'

In short, far from being simply an anodyne hero, Devushkin is also moody, unreliable, deceitful and vain, and the shame of his poverty occasionally seems about to drive him mad. In certain respects, he can even be seen as the first in Dostoevsky's long line of autobiographical figures. There are, of course, important differences in their age and position, yet many of the young author's comments in letters of the time bear a comical resemblance to those of Devushkin. Dostoevsky is just as obsessively worried about money and just as extravagant, just as anxious about status and quick to sense humiliation – qualities which were to be greatly magnified and elaborated in Golyadkin, protagonist of his next novel, *The Double*.

Dostoevsky had worked hard at *Poor People*, writing and rewriting several times; at one point he complained to his brother, '[It] has given me so much trouble that, if I had realised beforehand, I would never have got started on it at all.' His hard work shows in the sophisticated structure of the novel: an incomplete bundle of letters – hastily scribbled or long and discursive, some written in a flurry, two to a day, others after a gap of two or three weeks. In the gap between the two contrasting voices, each with their own anxieties and secrets, through the mass of detail and apparently random digressions, the reader senses his way towards the truth. 'They find my novel drawn out, when it doesn't contain one unnecessary word…' Dostoevsky went on. 'I go deep down and, digging it up, atom by atom, I uncover the whole…'

'The whole' in this case is a passionate, painfully detailed account of poverty and its effects on the human character. The poor that Dostoevsky describes are not particularly worthy or noble; they are as vain, silly and moody as the rest of us. Yet his ability to make us feel their humiliations and the knife-edge of survival that they tread is his great, humanising genius. It is no surprise, but a joy all the same to find that this gift was present even in his earliest fiction.

– Charlotte Hobson, 2002

Note:

All extracts from letters are taken from *The Selected Letters of Fyodor Dostoevsky*, edited by Joseph Frank and David I. Goldstein, London 1987.

In her letter dated July 1st the heroine of this short novel uses a Russian phrase which is ultimately untranslatable, the insurmountable difficulty lying in the two alternative meanings of the word *dobro*, both of which make sense in the context. The phrase either means 'to do good' or 'to create wealth'. As well as setting a frustrating puzzle for the translator, this ambiguity – which is suggestively combined with the word *selo*, 'village', in the heroine's surname too – encapsulates the mixture of social and spiritual themes in Dostoevsky's first published work in much the same way as does the title. For – thankfully just as in English too this time – the Russian adjective *bedny*, 'poor', can imply both material poverty and spiritual, moral hardship, either of which conditions might provoke pity.

The most obvious level on which the novel operates is probably that of the crusading social manifesto. Dostoevsky depicts protagonists who exist in penury in the hard heart of a nineteenth-century metropolis. The reader cannot help but be moved by the plight of Varvara Dobroselova and Makar Devushkin, authors of the letters that form the bulk of the text, as well as of the other figures, such as Gorshkov and Pokrovsky, whose stories echo to one degree or another those of the central characters. Certainly this was the main reason for the critical acclaim the work initially attracted. But the author equally shows that material comfort is not all a human being needs to achieve spiritual peace. One of the ironies of the closing pages is that just as things seem to be improving materially for a number of the characters, so the spiritual fabric of their lives comes apart. The welfare state can provide people with a decent income, accommodation, an education, but not with the less tangible factors that arguably contribute still more to contentment such as requited love, the respect of other men, or a sense of personal dignity. 'What's honour, my dear,' asks the hack novelist Ratazyayev, 'when you have nothing to eat?' The great novelist Dostoevsky would without doubt reply: 'A good deal.'

Yet as well as functioning on these social and spiritual planes, *Poor People* is a work much concerned with things literary. Indeed, a proper understanding of Dostoevsky's purpose is impossible without some knowledge of the literary context, for the work is highly allusive in its content. The title itself is a clear reference to the best-known story by Nikolai Karamzin, belletrist and historian, the man lauded by Alexander Pushkin in 1822 as Russia's finest writer of prose. *Poor Liza*, published in 1792 was his best-selling sentimental tale of the seduction and abandonment by a well-connected young man of an innocent peasant girl. The sad story ends with her suicide and the tears of the compassionate reader. Pushkin's praise for Karamzin was modified by his recognition of the dearth of competition in prose fiction, but by the 1830s the great poet had dethroned his predecessor by producing outstanding short stories of his own. In *The Queen of Spades* Pushkin created his own 'poor Liza', an orphaned ward who is jilted without even being seduced, yet finally makes a profitable marriage. Before this, however, Pushkin had already published *The Tales of Belkin*, a collection which in *Poor People* is sent by Varvara to Devushkin, arousing his great enthusiasm for the story *The Stationmaster*. What Devushkin does not realise as he praises the authenticity of Pushkin's portrait of one of life's 'humiliated and insulted', is that Pushkin was here giving an ironic rereading of Karamzin. Pushkin has 'poor Dunya', the daughter of the eponymous stationmaster, quite willingly seduced by a wealthy young man, but this time there is no abandonment; rather it is Dunya's father, assuming she will come to a bad end, who turns to drink and dies. Devushkin's delight at the story is prompted by his recognition of himself in the figure of the stationmaster and by the sympathy the latter elicits from the narrator. But being an unsophisticated reader, Devushkin does not appreciate all the parallels between the situations of Dunya and his own protégée, Varvara, and he certainly does not understand the irony in Pushkin's depiction of tragic delusion.

The other work that has a profound effect on Devushkin is Gogol's short story *The Greatcoat*. Here too he recognises a portrait of himself in the figure of the impecunious copying-clerk who is obliged at the cost of great hardship to buy a new coat to keep out the winter cold of St Petersburg. Unfortunately this adored new possession is immediately stolen, the clerk's feeble plea to his superior for justice is cruelly rejected, and after a brief delirium filled with unseemly language and insubordination, the sad creature dies. While Devushkin fails to grasp all the moral issues raised by this complex tale, he clearly recognises the way the clerk Bashmachkin (his name based on a Russian word meaning 'shoe') is mocked by both his peers and the narrator. He naively supposes that the author has spied on him, and is amazed that his own superior has allowed such a scurrilous work to be published.

Had he been one of Dostoevsky's readers, Devushkin would presumably have been much happier with the way that the younger writer presented a poor copying-clerk, for in *Poor People* Dostoevsky clearly intended to make a polemical response to *The Greatcoat*. The thrust of his new, more sympathetic approach lay in the humanisation of his central protagonist, along with a more realistic depiction of his situation. Gogol's Bashmachkin spends the bare minimum until the purchase of the fateful greatcoat, so why is he penniless? Dostoevsky's Devushkin uses most of his income either on supporting and entertaining Varvara, or on drowning his sorrows. Bashmachkin's love is for a mere item of clothing, Devushkin's is for a friendless orphan. Even their names are contrasting, Gogol's degrading derivation from *bashmak*, 'shoe', giving way to Dostoevsky's sympathetic derivation from *devushka*, 'young girl' (also contrasted in the novel with the name of the odious Bykov, 'Mr Bull'). Perhaps most importantly of all, Dostoevsky gives the humble copying-clerk a voice. Bashmachkin is scarcely able to form a coherent sentence and his writing never progresses beyond the stage of copying official documents. By contrast, Devushkin, who enjoys copying works of literature too, is moreover a writer himself, the author of letters to his beloved Varvara, a man who muses on his own potential as a writer and takes pride in the development of his prose style.

Not that he writes well. His prose, even at its best, is littered with the meaningless particles that typify the speech of Gogol's character too, and his generally unsophisticated, colloquial language is enriched only by occasional elements of bureaucratic jargon or purple prose that he has picked up in the course of his copying tasks. When he is agitated or drunk, his language at times deteriorates to the point of incoherence. Gogol and others had already used non-literary narrators to good effect before Dostoevsky, but the latter's sustained and psychologically grounded deployment of his character's voice was unprecedented and remains a brilliant achievement.

Unlike Devushkin's, Varvara's writing is generally controlled and relatively educated in style, yet nonetheless at times betrays her youth, with its emotional outbursts, self-absorption and impulsiveness. She is a more discerning reader than her friend and is already a practised writer before their correspondence begins: indeed her memoirs of her idyllic childhood in the country and first hard years in the city might even suggest literary aspirations at a time when female writers were just beginning to make their mark in Russia.

A further voice heard in the novel, albeit an insincere one, is that of Ratazyayev, extracts from whose writings are paraded by the admiring Devushkin. Dostoevsky has Ratazyayev imitating the comic style of Gogol as well as the manner of the society tale and the historical novel, each spiced up with touches of the overblown Romanticism then recently in vogue in Russia. His praise for these passages again demonstrates Devushkin's naivety, and they are amusing pastiches in themselves, but they also hint briefly at how the central relationships of *Poor People* might have been presented in the literary styles of the previous decade. Dostoevsky demonstrated his rejection of such clichéd forms by turning back further still beyond Romantic fashion and reviving the epistolary novel, simultaneously refreshing the outdated genre by having as correspondents not the customary idle, educated aristocrats, but poverty-stricken tenement-dwellers.

In general, the epistolary form more readily associated with the eighteenth century here disguises a novel with concerns very much of Dostoevsky's own age. Complex psychological insights accompany acute social observation in an oppressive urban environment – St Petersburg itself is a vital element in a story which could not have been set elsewhere – in a way that in many respects prefigures his great novels of the 1860s and beyond. *Poor People* reveals a youthful Dostoevsky making a debut that owed much to what had gone before in Russian culture, but at the same time offering tantalising glimpses of the mature artist who would profoundly influence much of what was to follow him throughout the literary world.

– *Hugh Aplin, 2002*

Poor People

Oh, I'm fed up with these storytellers!
Rather than write something improving, nice,
something that makes you feel good, they insist
on digging up all the dirt from under the ground!...
They ought to be banned from writing!
I mean, whatever is it like: you're reading...
and you unwittingly fall into thought –
and then all sorts of rubbish comes into your head;
truly, I would ban them from writing;
I really would ban them altogether.[1]

– *Prince V.F. Odoevsky*

My priceless Varvara Alexeyevna!

Yesterday I was happy, exceedingly happy, impossibly happy! For just once in your life, you stubborn girl, you did as I asked. In the evening, at about eight o'clock, I wake up (you know, my dear, how I like to have a little sleep for an hour or two after work), I've got out a candle, I'm getting the papers ready, sharpening my quill, and suddenly, by chance, I raise my eyes – and truly, my heart just leaped! So you really did understand what it was I wanted, what my little heart wanted! I see the corner of the curtain at your window is folded back and attached to the pot of balsam in just exactly the way I was hinting to you that time; and straight away it seemed to me that your little face appeared for a moment at the window too, and that you too were looking in my direction from your little room, that you too were thinking of me. And how upset I was, sweetheart, that I couldn't get a good look at your pretty little face! There was a time when we could see clearly too, my dear. It's no fun getting old! Even now everything looks blurred to my eyes; you just do a little bit of work in the evening, do a bit of writing, and in the morning your eyes are all red, and you have tears running so that you even feel ashamed sometimes in front of strangers. But anyway, in my imagination your little smile simply shone out, my little angel, your kind, friendly smile; and in my heart there was just the same feeling as that time I kissed you, Varenka – do you remember, my little angel? Do you know, sweetheart, it even seemed to me that you wagged your finger at me? Is that right, you naughty girl? Be sure to describe it all in lots of detail in your letter.

Well, and what about our little idea for your curtain, Varenka? It's really nice, isn't it? Whether I'm sitting working, or going to bed, or waking up, I know for sure that you're thinking of me over there too, you remember me, and you're well and cheerful yourself. If you lower the curtain, that means – 'Goodbye, Makar Alexeyevich, it's time for bed!' If you raise it, that means – 'Good morning, Makar Alexeyevich, how did you sleep', or – 'How are you health-wise, Makar Alexeyevich? So far as I'm concerned, thank God, I'm healthy and well!' You see, my poppet, how well thought out it all is; and you don't need any letters!

Cunning, isn't it? And the idea was mine, you know! What do you think, am I good at this sort of thing, Varvara Alexeyevna?

I can report to you, my dear, Varvara Alexeyevna, that I slept this last night in good order, contrary to expectations, and I'm very pleased about that; although in new accommodation, when you've just moved in, it's never easy to sleep somehow; there's always something that's not quite right! I got up this morning fresh as a daisy – it was a real pleasure! What a lovely morning it was today, my dear! Our window was wide open; the sun's shining, the little birds are chirping, the air is full of the smells of spring, and the whole of nature is coming to life – well, and everything else was in accordance too; everything in order, spring-like. I even did quite a nice little bit of dreaming today, and all my dreams were about you, Varenka. I compared you with a little bird of the heavens, created for the pleasure of men and the adornment of nature. And then, Varenka, I thought that we too, people who live in care and worry, should also envy the carefree and innocent happiness of the birds of the heavens – well, and all the rest likewise, and the same; that is, I kept making such remote comparisons. I've got this book, Varenka, and it's got the same stuff in it, all the same things described in real detail. Why I'm writing is that there are different dreams, you know, my dear. And now it's spring, so my ideas too are always so nice, sharp, inventive, and the dreams I have are tender; everything is rose-coloured. That's why I've written all this; but actually I got all this from the book. In it the author discloses the same desire in verse and writes: 'Why not a bird am I, a predatory bird!'

Well, etc. There are various other ideas there too, but so be it! Where was it you went this morning, though, Varvara Alexeyevna? I wasn't yet getting ready to go to work, but you, just like a little spring birdie, you fluttered out of your room and crossed the courtyard so nice and cheerful. How cheerful I felt looking at you! Ah, Varenka, Varenka! Don't be sad; tears can't help your grief; that I know, my dear, that I know from experience. You're so at peace now, and you're a little better in your health. Well, how's your Fedora? Ah, what a kind woman she is! Write to me, Varenka, about what it's like living there with her now and about whether you're happy with everything. Fedora can be a bit grumpy, but pay no attention to that, Varenka. So be it! She's so kind.

I've already written to you about Tereza here – a kind and true woman as well. But how worried I was about our letters! How would they be passed on? And then to our good fortune the Lord went and sent Tereza. She's a kind woman, meek, silent. But our landlady is pitiless. She keeps her working like an old rag or something.

Well, and what a dump I've ended up in, Varvara Alexeyevna! Well, what accommodation! After all, I lived the life of a hermit before, as you know, peaceful and quiet; sometimes there'd be a fly in my room and you could hear it flying. But here there's noise, shouting, uproar! You don't know how everything's arranged here yet though, do you? Imagine something like a long corridor, utterly dark and dirty. Along its right-hand side is a blank wall, while on the left there's door after door, like hotel-rooms, all stretching out in a row. Well, and people rent these sort of hotel-rooms, and in each of them there's a single room, and people live sometimes two, sometimes three to a room. Don't ask about order – it's like Noah's ark! But actually they seem to be good people, all the educated, learned type. There's one civil servant (his job's something to do with literature), he's a well-read man; he talks about Homer, and about Brambeus[2], and about various authors of theirs, he talks about everything – he's a clever man! There are two officers living here and they're always playing cards. A midshipman lives here; and an English teacher lives here. Hang on, I'll amuse you, my dear; I'll describe them in a future letter satirically, that is, what they're like individually, in full detail. Our landlady – a very small, dirty, nasty old woman – goes about all day wearing shoes and a housecoat and keeps shouting all day at Tereza. I live in the kitchen, although it will be much more correct to put it like this: there is one room here alongside the kitchen (and you should note that our kitchen is clean, bright and very nice), a small room, a modest little corner… that is, to put it even better, the kitchen is large, with three windows, and along the perpendicular wall I have a partition, so that it works out as if there were another room, a supernumerary room; everything's spacious, convenient, and there's a window and everything – in a word, everything's convenient. Well, that's my little corner. Well, and don't you go thinking, my dear, that there might be something else going on and there might be some secret significance; that, you know, a kitchen! That is, perhaps I do

7

indeed live in this room behind the partition, but that's alright; I live separately from everyone else, in a small way, nice and quiet. I've put a bed in my room, a table, a chest of drawers, a couple of chairs, I've hung up an icon. True, there is accommodation that's better – maybe much better – but convenience is the main thing; after all, I've done it all for convenience, and don't you go thinking it's for anything else. Your little window is opposite, across the courtyard; and the courtyard's narrow, I can see you passing – it's much more cheerful for hapless old me, and cheaper too. The worst room here, with board, costs thirty-five paper roubles. I can't afford it! But my accommodation costs me seven paper roubles, and board is five silver roubles: that's twenty-four roubles and fifty kopeks, whereas I was paying exactly thirty before, but had to deny myself a lot of things; I didn't always drink tea, but now I've saved enough for tea and for sugar. You know, my dear, it's shameful somehow not drinking tea; the people here are all well-to-do, so it's shameful. For the sake of other people you drink it, Varenka, for show, for tone; but it's all the same to me, I'm not choosy. Put it like this: will there be much left for pocket money – you always need some: well, there's boots and clothes? And that's my whole salary. I don't complain, I'm satisfied. It's enough. It's been enough for several years now; there are bonuses sometimes too. Well, goodbye, my angel. I bought a couple of pots of balsam and a geranium – cheaply. Perhaps you like mignonette? There's mignonette too, you just write; yes, write about everything in as much detail as possible, you know? And by the way, don't go thinking anything and having doubts, my dear, about me and my renting a room like this. No, it was convenience that made me do it, and convenience alone that seduced me. I mean, I'm saving money, my dear, putting it aside; I've got a little money. Pay no attention to the fact that I'm so quiet, that I look as if a fly could break me with its wing. No, my dear, I'm nobody's fool, and my character is absolutely as it should be in a man of a firm and placid nature. Goodbye, my angel! I've covered almost two whole sheets in writing to you, and should have gone to work ages ago. I kiss your fingers, my dear, and remain

Your most humble servant and most faithful friend

Makar Devushkin

PS One request: reply, my angel, in as much detail as possible. I'm sending you a pound of sweets with this, Varenka; you eat them for your health, and for God's sake don't worry about me and don't hold anything against me. Well, so it's goodbye then, my dear.

8TH APRIL

Dear Sir, Makar Alexeyevich!
Do you know that I shall finally be obliged to fall out with you completely? I swear to you, kind Makar Alexeyevich, that it is even onerous for me to accept your gifts. I know what they cost you, what deprivations, and how you deny yourself the most essential things. How many times have I told you that I need nothing, absolutely nothing; that I don't have the power to reward you even for those benefactions that you have scattered upon me up until now? And why do I need these pots? Well, the balsam may be another matter, but why the geranium? One only has to say a single incautious little word, like about this geranium, for example, and you are sure to buy it straight away; and it's probably expensive, isn't it? How delightful the flowers on it are! Crimson with little crosses. Where did you find such a pretty geranium? I've put it in the middle of the window where it can best be seen; and on the floor I'll put a bench, and on the bench I'll put some more flowers; only let me get rich myself! Fedora is quite overjoyed; it's like paradise in our room now – clean and bright! Well, and why the sweets? And truly, I guessed at once from your letter that something was wrong with you – paradise, and spring, and fragrances flying about, and birds chirping. What's this, I thought, surely there won't be verse here as well? For it really is true, verse is the one thing that's lacking in your letter, Makar Alexeyevich! Tender feelings, and rose-coloured dreams – it's all there! I didn't even think about the curtain; it must have got hooked up itself when I was rearranging the pots; there you are!

Ah, Makar Alexeyevich! Whatever you say, however you calculate your income to deceive me, to demonstrate that absolutely all of it is spent on you alone, still you cannot conceal or hide anything from me. It's clear that you deprive yourself of essentials because of me.

9

Whatever put it into your head, for example, to rent such accommodation? After all, people disturb you, trouble you; it's cramped and inconvenient. You like privacy, but that's just what you don't have around you there! And you could live much better, judging by your salary. Fedora says that previously you used to live better by far than now. Surely you haven't lived all your life like this, in solitude, in deprivation, without joy, without a friendly, affable word, renting corners from strangers? Ah, how sorry I feel for you, kind friend! At least take pity on your health, Makar Alexeyevich! You say your eyes are getting weak, so don't write by candlelight; why do you write? Your zeal for your work is doubtless well-known to your superiors in any case.

Once again I beg you, don't spend so much money on me. I know you love me, but you're not rich yourself… I too was cheerful when I got up today. I felt so well; Fedora had already been at work for a long time and had got some work for me. I was so pleased; I just went to buy some silk, then I started work. The whole of the morning my soul felt so light, I was so cheerful! But now it's dark thoughts all the time again, I'm sad; my heart aches through and through.

Ah, what is going to happen to me, what will be my fate? The hard thing is that I am in such uncertainty, that I have no future, that I cannot even foresee what will become of me. It's frightening just looking back. There's such grief everywhere there that my heart is torn in two at the memory alone. I shall forever bemoan those wicked people that ruined me!

It's getting dark. Time for work. I should like to write to you of many things, but there's no time, there's a deadline for the work. I need to hurry. Of course letters are a good thing; everything's less dull. But why do you never come to visit us yourself? Why is that, Makar Alexeyevich? After all, it's not far for you now, and you sometimes have some free time set aside. Please come and visit us! I've seen your Tereza. She looks so ill; I felt sorry for her; I gave her twenty kopeks. Yes! I almost forgot: be sure to write everything in as much detail as possible about your daily life. What are the people around you like, and do you get on well with them? I want to know all this very much. Look out now, be sure to write! And today I shall fold the corner back on purpose. Go to bed early; yesterday I saw your light burning until midnight. Well, goodbye. I'm depressed today, and I'm bored and sad! Evidently, it's just one of those days! Goodbye.

Your

Varvara Dobroselova

Madam, Varvara Alexeyevna!

Yes, sweetheart, yes, my dear, evidently it was one of those days that befell sad old me! Yes, you had a joke at the expense of this old man, Varvara Alexeyevna! Actually it's my fault, it's all my fault! I shouldn't have set out on love affairs and double entendres in my old age, with just a wisp of hair left… And another thing, my dear: a man's a funny thing sometimes, a very funny thing. Oh, Saints alive, the things he'll talk about and come out with at times! And what's the result, what follows from it? Nothing at all follows and the result is such rubbish that may the Lord preserve me! I'm not angry, my dear, I'm not, but it's just upsetting to remember everything, upsetting that I wrote to you so ornately and stupidly. And I went off to work today strutting like a peacock; there was such radiance in my heart. For no reason at all there was such festivity in my soul; I felt cheerful! I started work on my papers assiduously – and what was the result of it later on! It was only later on when I looked around that everything became as it was before – grey and gloomy. Still those same ink-stains, still those same desks and papers, and me too still the same; so, I was exactly the same as I had been – so what reason was there to have been riding around on Pegasus? And where had it all come from? Because the sun had peeped through and the sky had turned azure! Was that why? And what are these fragrances, considering the things that turn up under the windows in our courtyard! Evidently it all seemed that way to me because of my foolishness. But after all, it does sometimes happen that a man can get lost in his own feelings like that and talk nonsense. It occurs for no other reason than the excessive, stupid enthusiasm of the heart. I didn't walk home, but plodded; for no reason at all my head began aching; it was evidently just one thing leading to another. (Maybe the wind got into my back.) I was delighted by the spring, like a complete idiot, and I went out in my thin greatcoat. And you were wrong about my feelings, my dear! You took their outpouring completely the wrong way. It was fatherly affection that inspired me, pure, fatherly affection alone, Varvara Alexeyevna; for I take the place of your real father, by reason of your bitter orphanhood; I say this from my soul, from the bottom of my heart, as a relative. Because whichever way you look at it, even if I am only a distant relation, maybe, as the saying goes, only a third cousin twice removed, still I am a relative nonetheless, and now your closest relative and protector; for in the closest place of all where you had the right to look for protection and defence, you found betrayal and injury. And regarding the verse, I'll say to you, my dear, that it's indecent for me, in my old age, to exercise myself in the composition of poetry. Poetry is poppycock! Even in schools nowadays they thrash the boys for writing verse… there you are, my dear.

What is it you write me, Varvara Alexeyevna, about convenience, about peace and about various other things? My dear, I'm not a grumbler and I'm not demanding, I've never lived better than I do now; so why should I be choosy in my old age? I'm well-fed, clothed and shod; and who are we to start getting big ideas? We're not from a family of counts! My father's job didn't give him the status of a nobleman, and considering all his family he had a smaller income than me. I'm no mollycoddle! Actually, if it's a matter of truth, then in my old accommodation everything was far better; it was a bit freer, my dear. Of course, my present accommodation is good as well, even in a certain way more cheerful and, if you like, more varied; I'm not saying anything against it, but still I feel regret about the old place. We old people, the elderly that is, get used to our old things as if they were part of the family. The place was just a little one; you know, the walls were… well, what can you say! – the walls were like any other walls, they're not the point, but it's the memories of everything in my past that make me feel depressed… It's a funny thing – it's hard, but it's as if the memories were pleasant. Even what was bad, what I even got upset about at times, in my memories even that is somehow cleansed of the bad part and stands before my imagination in an attractive form. We lived quietly, Varenka; my landlady, the old lady, now deceased, and I. And now I recall even my old lady with a sad feeling! She was a good woman and didn't charge a lot for my lodgings. She was always knitting blankets out of various old scraps on needles a yard long; that's all she ever did. We shared the same light together, so we worked at the one table. She had a granddaughter, Masha – I remember her when she was still a child – she'll be a girl of about thirteen now. She was such a mischievous little girl, cheerful, always making us laugh; and so it was that we lived, the three of us. On a long winter's night we used to sit down at the round table, drink some tea and then set about our work. And so that Masha wouldn't get bored and misbehave, the little scamp, the old lady used to start telling tales. And what tales they were! Even a clever, intelligent man would have listened intently, let alone a child. Why, I myself sometimes used to light up my pipe and listen so intently that I'd even forget about my work. And the child, our mischievous little girl, would fall into thought; she'd prop up her pink cheek with her little hand, open her pretty little mouth wide, and as soon as there was a frightening story she'd squeeze up tight against the old lady. And it was nice for us watching her; and you didn't notice the candle burning down, and at times you didn't hear either the blizzard raging or the snowstorm whirling outside. We lived well, Varenka; and that was the way we lived together for almost twenty years. But why am I rambling on here? Perhaps you don't like such material, and it's not so easy for me to remember it, especially now: it's twilight time. Tereza's busy with something or other, my head's aching, and my back aches a little as well, and my thoughts are so odd, it's as if they were aching too; I feel sad today, Varenka! And what's this you write, my dear? How can I come and visit you? Sweetheart, whatever will people say? After all, I'll have to cross the courtyard, the people here will notice me, they'll start asking questions – rumours will start, gossip will start, the business will be given a different meaning. No, my angel, it'll be better if I see you at the service tomorrow night; that'll be wiser and safer for both of us. Now don't be hard on me, my dear, for my writing you a letter like this; now I've read it through I can see that it's all rather incoherent. I'm an old man, Varenka, with no education; I didn't complete my studies when I was young, and now, if I should start studying again, my brain won't take anything in. I confess, my dear, I've no talent for description, and I know, without anyone else pointing it out and mocking, that if I want to write anything a little bit more involved, then I'll come out with a lot of nonsense. I saw you by the window today, saw you lowering the blind. Goodbye, goodbye, may the Lord keep you! Goodbye, Varvara Alexeyevna.

Your selfless friend

Makar Devushkin

PS My dear, I'm not writing any satires on anyone now. I've grown too old, my dear, Varvara Alexeyevna, to bare my teeth to no purpose! And people will start laughing at me on the basis of the Russian proverb: whoever, as they say, lays a trap for somebody else... falls into it himself.

9TH APRIL

Dear Sir, Makar Alexeyevich!

Well, you should be ashamed of yourself, my friend and benefactor, Makar Alexeyevich, becoming so sorrowful and capricious. Surely you haven't taken offence! Oh, I can often be incautious, but I didn't expect you to take my words as a cutting joke. Be assured that I shall never dare to laugh at your age or your character. This all happened because of my frivolity, or rather because of my dreadful boredom, and when you're bored, what won't you start doing? I assumed that in your letter you yourself wanted to have a joke. I became dreadfully sad when I saw that you were unhappy with me. No, my dear friend and benefactor, you'll be mistaken if you suspect me of insensitivity and ingratitude. In my heart I can appreciate all you've done for me, defending me from wicked people, from their persecution and hatred. I shall always pray to God on your behalf, and if my prayer reaches God, and Heaven pays heed to it, then you will be happy.

I feel very unwell today. I'm feverish and shivering by turns. Fedora is very worried about me. There's no reason for you to feel ashamed about visiting us, Makar Alexeyevich. What is it to anyone else? You're acquainted with us, and that's all there is to it!... Goodbye, Makar

Alexeyevich. There's nothing more to write about at the moment, and I can't anyway: I'm dreadfully unwell. I beg you once more not to be angry with me and to be confident in the eternal respect and in the attachment

With which I have the honour to be your most devoted

And most humble servant

Varvara Dobroselova

Madam, Varvara Alexeyevna!

Ah, my dear, what's the matter with you? I mean, you scare me like this every time. I write to you in every letter that you should look after yourself, that you should wrap up warm, that you shouldn't go out when the weather's bad, that you should observe caution in all things – but, my little angel, you don't do as I say. Ah, sweetheart, it's as if you were some child! You're weak, you know, weak as a straw, I know it. Just a little bit of a breeze, and you're sure to be poorly. So you need to be careful, make an effort on your own behalf, avoid dangers and not bring your friends to grief and despondency.

You express a desire, my dear, to learn in detail about my everyday life and about everything that surrounds me. I gladly make haste to fulfil your desire, my dear. I'll begin at the beginning: it'll be more orderly. Firstly, at the front entrance of our house the staircases are very smart; especially the main one – clean, bright, wide, all cast-iron and mahogany. But then don't even ask about the backstairs: winding, damp, dirty, with the steps broken and the walls so greasy that your arm sticks if you lean on them. On every landing there are broken chests, chairs and cupboards, rags are hung up everywhere, the windows are knocked out; there are tubs with all sorts of muck, dirt, rubbish, egg-shells and fish-sounds; there's a bad smell… in a word, it's unpleasant.

I've already described the layout of the rooms to you; you can't argue, it's convenient, that's true, but they're stuffy somehow, that is it's not so much that they smell bad, but, if I can put it like this, there's a rather mouldy, pungently sweet sort of smell. The first impression is

15

unfavourable, but that's alright; you only have to be here a couple of minutes, and then it passes, and you don't even notice it passing, because you somehow start to smell bad yourself, and your clothes start to smell, and your hands start to smell, and everything starts to smell – well, and you get used to it. The canaries keep on dying here. The midshipman's already bought five – they can't live in our air, that's all there is to it. Our kitchen is large, spacious and bright. True, it's a little smoky in the mornings when people are frying fish or beef, and they do spill liquids and make it wet everywhere, but on the other hand it's a real paradise in the evening. There's always old linen hanging on lines in our kitchen; and since my room isn't far away, that is it almost adjoins the kitchen, the smell of the linen troubles me a little; but it's alright: you get used to it after you've lived here a while.

From first thing in the morning, Varenka, the hustle and bustle begins, people getting up, walking around, banging – it's everybody who needs to rising, the people who have jobs or just work for themselves; everybody starts drinking tea. The samovars here belong to the landlady for the most part, there aren't many of them, well so we all take turns; and whoever gets in with his teapot out of turn immediately gets his head bitten off. I almost went out of turn the first time, but… well, what's the point of writing about that! It was here that I got to know everyone. The midshipman was the first one I got to know; he's very frank, told me everything: about his father, about his mother, about his sister, who's married to the Tula district assessor, and about the town of Kronstadt. He promised to be my protector in all things and invited me to his room for tea straight away. I found him in that very room where they usually play cards here. They gave me some tea there, and insisted that I should play a game of chance with them. I don't know whether they were laughing at me or not; only they'd played the whole night through themselves, and when I went in they were still playing. There was chalk, and cards, and such smoke floating all around the room that it made my eyes smart. I wouldn't play with them, and I was immediately told off for talking philosophy. After that nobody even spoke to me at all the whole time, and to tell the truth, I was glad of it. I won't visit them now; it's gambling there, just gambling! But the civil servant who has something to do with literature also has gatherings in the evenings. Well, with him everything is nice and modest and innocent and tactful; all on a refined footing.

Well, Varenka, I'll remark to you in passing too that our landlady is a really vile woman, and what's more, a real witch. You've seen Tereza. Well, what is she, when it comes down to it? As thin as a plucked and sickly chicken. And there are only two servants in the house: Tereza and Faldoni,[3] the landlady's manservant. I don't know, perhaps he has some other name as well, only he answers to this one too; and that's what everybody calls him. He's ginger, looks like an Estonian, he's one-eyed, snub-nosed and rude; he's always rowing with Tereza, they almost come to blows. Speaking generally, it's not absolutely nice for me living here. To fall asleep straight away just like that at night and relax – it never happens. There are always sure to be people sitting gambling somewhere, and sometimes things even happen that it's shameful to relate. Now I've got used to it a little after all, but all the same I wonder at how people with families manage, living in such an uproar. An entire family of poor people of some sort rents a room from our landlady, only not alongside the other rooms, but on the other side, in the corner, set apart. Quiet people! Nobody even hears anything of them. They live in one small room divided by a partition. He's some sort of civil servant without a post, dismissed from the service for some reason about seven years ago. His name's Gorshkov; a grey-haired little man; he goes around in such soiled, such worn clothing that it's painful to see; far worse than mine! He's a pitiful, puny thing (we meet sometimes in the corridor); his knees shake, his hands shake, his head shakes, perhaps it's some illness or other, God knows; he's timid, afraid of everyone, slips by to one side; I know I can be shy at times, but he's even worse. His family is a wife and three children. The eldest, a boy, is just like his father, he's a sickly one too. The wife was once not at all bad-looking, you can see that even now; the poor thing goes around in such pitiful rags. I've heard they're in debt to the landlady; she's not that kind with them somehow. I've also heard that Gorshkov himself has problems of some sort, and it was on account of them he lost his job… there may be a court case, he may be on trial, or he may be under some investigation or something – I can't tell you for sure. But they're poor, poor – oh Lord God! Their room is always quiet and silent, as if nobody's even living there. You don't even hear the children. And it's just never the case that children don't get a bit frisky and play about once in a while, so that's a bad sign for sure. Once I happened to be passing by their doors in the evening for some reason; at that moment the building had become unusually quiet somehow; I hear a whimpering, then a whispering, then again a whimpering, just as if someone were crying, but so quietly, so pitifully, that my heart was quite torn apart, and afterwards the thought of those poor people stayed with me the whole night through, so that I didn't even manage to get to sleep properly.

Well, goodbye, my priceless little friend Varenka! I've described everything to you as well as I know how. I've been thinking only about you all day today. My heart's quite despondent about you, my dear. I mean, I know, my poppet, you have no warm coat. Oh, how tired I am of these Petersburg springs, wind and rain with a bit of snow mixed in – it'll be the death of me, Varenka! Such a healthy climate, that may the Lord preserve me! Don't be hard on my writing, poppet; there's no style, Varenka, no style whatsoever. If only there were some! I write whatever comes into my head, just so as to cheer you up with something. I mean, if I'd had a bit of schooling, it'd be a different matter; but after all, what sort did I get? Not even a poor boy's schooling.

Your eternal and faithful friend

Makar Devushkin

Dear Sir, Makar Alexeyevich!

I met my cousin Sasha today! It's terrible! She'll be ruined too, the poor thing! I also heard talk that Anna Fyodorovna is continually trying to find things out about me. It seems she'll never stop tormenting me. She says she wants *to forgive me*, to forget everything in the past, and that she'll be sure to visit me herself. She says you're not my relative at all, that she's a closer relation, that you have no right whatsoever to enter into our family relationships, and that it's shameful and indecent for me to live on your charity and to be kept by you… She says I've forgotten her hospitality, that she may have saved mother and me from starving to death, that she gave us our food and drink and spent money on us for more than two and a half years, that on top of all that she waived our debt. She didn't want to spare my mother either! But if my poor mother knew what they'd done to me! God sees!… Anna Fyodorovna says that in my stupidity I didn't know how to hold onto my good fortune, that she was herself leading me towards that good fortune, that she isn't to blame for anything else, and that I didn't know how to stand up for my honour myself, or perhaps didn't even want to do so. Who then is to blame for all this, great God! She says that Mr Bykov is absolutely right, and you don't marry just anyone who… oh, what's the point of writing! It's cruel to hear such lies, Makar Alexeyevich! I don't know what's happening to me now. I'm shaking, crying, sobbing; I've been two hours writing you this letter. I thought she would at least admit her blame before me; and that's the way she is now! For God's sake don't be alarmed, my friend, my only well-wisher! Fedora exaggerates everything: I'm not ill. I only caught a bit of a cold yesterday when I went to the Volkovo cemetery for the memorial service for my mother. Why didn't you come with me? I begged you so. Ah, my poor, poor mother, if you were to rise from the grave, if you knew, if you could see what they've done to me!…

V. D.

20TH MAY

My sweet Varenka!

I'm sending you a few grapes, poppet; they're good for someone convalescing, they say, and the doctor recommends them for quenching your thirst, so they're just solely for your thirst. You had a fancy for some roses the other day, my dear; so here I am now sending you them. Have you any appetite, poppet? That's the main thing. Anyway, thank God that everything's over and done with and that our misfortunes are coming to an end completely too. We shall give thanks to Heaven! But as far as a book is concerned, I can't get hold of one anywhere for the time being. They say there is one book here that's good and written in a very elevated style; they say it's good, I haven't read it myself, but they really praise it here. I asked for it for myself; they've promised to pass it on. But will you read it? You're a choosy one in that respect; it's hard to satisfy your taste, I know you, sweetheart. You probably want poetry all the time, lamentations, amours – well, I'll get hold of some poetry too, I'll get hold of the lot; there's a notebook with things copied into it.

I'm doing fine. Don't you worry about me, please, my dear. And the things that Fedora told you about me, that's all nonsense; you tell her that she lied, be sure to tell her, the rumour-monger!... I haven't sold my new uniform at all; and why should I, just think about it, why should I sell it? I mean, they say I'm due forty silver roubles in bonuses, so why on earth should I sell it? Don't you worry, my dear. She's a suspicious one, that Fedora, suspicious. Our life's just beginning, sweetheart! Only you must get better, my angel, for God's sake get better and don't upset an old man. Who is it telling you I've got thin? It's slander, slander again! I'm fighting fit and I've grown so fat that I'm becoming ashamed of myself, I'm well-fed and perfectly content; but if you would only get better! Well, goodbye, my angel; I kiss all your fingers and remain

Your eternal, unchanging friend

Makar Devushkin

PS Oh my poppet, what's this you've started writing again after all?... What are these mad ideas! How can I possibly visit you so often, my dear, how can I? I ask you. Only by making use of the darkness at night; and nowadays there's hardly any night to speak of: it's that time of the year. As it is, my dear, my angel, I hardly left you at all the whole of the time you were ill, while you were delirious; but here too I'm not even sure myself how I managed all those things; and even so I stopped visiting afterwards; for people started getting inquisitive and asking a lot of questions. Some sort of gossip has started spreading here already without that. I'm relying on Tereza; she doesn't chatter; but all the same, think about it for yourself, my dear, what will it be like when they find everything out about us? What'll they think and what'll they say then? So you be brave, my dear, and wait until you're better; and then we'll be able to have a rendezvous somewhere out of doors.

Dearest Makar Alexeyevich!

I do so want to do something nice and pleasing for you in return for all your trouble and effort over me, all your love for me, so I finally resolved when I was bored to dig through my chest of drawers and root out my notebook, which I'm now indeed sending you. I began it during the happy period of my life. You've often shown curiosity, asking questions about my former way of life, about my mother, about Pokrovsky, about my stay with Anna Fyodorovna and, finally, about my recent misfortunes, and you were so impatient in your desire to read this notebook, where I took it into my head, God knows why, to record certain moments of my life, that I have no doubt my dispatch will bring you great pleasure. Yet for me it was sad somehow reading it through again. It seems to me that I've already doubled in age since I wrote the last line of these notes. It was all written at various times. Goodbye, Makar Alexeyevich! I'm dreadfully bored now, and I often suffer from insomnia. It's a very dull convalescence!

V. D.

1

I was only fourteen years old when my father died. My childhood was the happiest time of my life. It began not here, but far away, in the provinces, in the back of beyond. My father was steward on the huge estate of Prince P. in the province of T. We lived in one of the Prince's villages, and we lived peacefully, quietly, happily… I was such a lively little girl; all I ever used to do was run around the fields, the copses, the garden, and nobody even bothered about me. Father was constantly occupied with his work, mother was busy with her housekeeping; nobody gave me any lessons, and I was glad of it too. I used to run off first thing in the morning either to the pond, or to the copse, or to the haymaking, or to the reapers – and it didn't matter that the sun was burning, that you didn't know yourself where you'd run to from the village, you'd get all scratched on bushes, tear your dress – you'd be scolded at home afterwards, but that was nothing to me.

And I think I would have been happy like that, if I had even had to live in the one place and not move out of the village for the whole of my life. Yet even as a child I was forced to leave my native parts. I was still only twelve years old when we moved to St Petersburg. Ah, with what sadness do I recall our sorrowful preparations! How I cried as I bade farewell to everything that was so dear to me. I remember throwing myself onto my father's neck, and begging tearfully to stay in the village for just a little longer. My father shouted at me, my mother cried; she said it was necessary, that matters demanded it. Old Prince P. had died. The heirs had dismissed my father from his position. Father had a little money invested in the hands of private individuals in St Petersburg. Hoping to set his circumstances to rights, he considered his personal presence there essential. I learned all this later on from my mother. We settled here on the Petersburg Side and lived in the same place right up until my father's death.

How difficult it was for me to get used to my new life! We arrived in St Petersburg in the autumn. As we were leaving the village, the day was so bright, warm and brilliant; the farm work was drawing to a close; huge stacks of corn already towered up on the threshing-floors and raucous flocks of birds crowded around; everything was so clear and cheerful, but here, as we rode into the city, there was rain, the damp autumnal frost, foul weather, slush, and a crowd of new, unfamiliar faces, inhospitable, discontented, angry! Somehow or other we settled in. I remember everyone bustling around so at our new place, continually busy setting up the new home. Father was always out, and mother did not have a minute's peace – I was completely forgotten. I felt sad getting up in the morning after the first night in our new home. Our windows looked out onto some yellow fence. There was dirt in the street all the time. Passers-by were rare, and they were all so heavily wrapped up, everyone was so cold.

And at home there was terrible anguish and boredom for days on end. We had almost no relatives or close acquaintances. My father had fallen out with Anna Fyodorovna. (He owed her some money.) People visited us on business quite frequently. Usually they argued, made a noise, shouted. After each visit my father became so displeased, angry; he used to walk for hours on end from corner to corner, frowning, and would not say a word to anyone. Then my mother did not dare even to try to speak to him and remained silent. I would sit down in a corner somewhere with a book, meekly, quietly, not daring to move.

Three months after our arrival in St Petersburg I was sent to boarding-school. How sad I was at first among strangers! Everything was so dry and bleak – the governesses shrieked so, the girls were so mocking, and I was such a savage. Life was strict and exacting. Everything to a timetable, communal meals, boring teachers – all this was a torment, a torture to me at first. I could not even sleep there. I used to cry all through the night, the long, dull, cold night. In the evenings everyone would be revising or learning their lessons; I would be sitting there over dialogues or vocabulary, not daring to move, but actually thinking all the time about the corner that was our home, about my father, my mother, my old nanny and my nanny's fairy tales... ah, how sad I would feel! The most trivial little thing in the house, even that you remember with pleasure. You think and think: how nice it would be at home now! I would be sitting by the samovar in our little room together with the others; it would be so warm, nice and familiar. How I would hug mother now, you think, ever so close, ever so tight! You think and think, and you start crying quietly in your anguish, quelling the tears in your breast, and the vocabulary won't go into your head. And when you haven't learned a lesson for the following day, you dream all night about the teacher, madam, the girls; you try to memorise the lessons all night in your sleep, but the next day you know nothing. They make you kneel, give you only one meal. I was so cheerless and miserable. At first all the girls laughed at me, teased me, put me off when I was saying my lessons, pinched me when we filed in to lunch or tea, complained to a governess about me for no reason whatsoever. But what heaven when my nanny came to fetch me on a Saturday evening. I used to hug the dear old lady so in a transport of joy. She dressed me, wrapped me up, then could not keep pace with me on the way home as I kept chattering and chattering and telling her things. I arrived home cheerful, joyful, I hugged everyone close as if we had spent ten years apart. Talking would start, conversations, stories; you would greet everybody, laugh, chuckle, run around, jump about. Serious conversations would start with my father, about the sciences, about our teachers, about French, about Lomond's grammar – and we were all so cheerful, so content. Even now

I feel cheerful remembering those minutes. I tried with all my might to study and please my father. I could see he was giving up the last of everything for me, while God knows how he struggled himself. With every day he was becoming more gloomy, displeased, angry; his character was completely altered for the worse: his affairs were not going well, there were masses of debts. My mother was even afraid to cry at times, was afraid to say a word, in case she made my father angry; she made herself ill; she began getting thinner and thinner and developed a bad cough. Sometimes I came home from the boarding-school – such sad faces everywhere; mother crying quietly, father angry. Reproaches and recriminations would start. Father would start saying that I brought him no joy, no comfort; that because of me they were going without everything, yet I still couldn't speak French; in short, all the failures, all the misfortunes, everything, everything was vented on me and my mother. And how could he torment my poor mother? It was heart-breaking to look at her sometimes; her cheeks were hollow, her eyes sunken, there was this consumptive colour to her face. I came in for it most of all. It always began with trifles, and then God knows how far it would go; often I did not even understand what it was all about. What wasn't I held to account for!… There was French, the fact that I was a complete fool, the fact that the proprietor of our boarding-school was a negligent, stupid woman; the fact that she did not trouble herself about our morality; the fact that my father could still not find himself a position, and the fact that Lomond's grammar was a rotten grammar, and Zapolsky's was much better; the fact that a lot of money had been spent on me for nothing; the fact that I was evidently bereft of feelings, made of stone – in short, there was poor me, struggling with all my might, memorising dialogues and vocabulary, and I was to blame for everything, I was responsible for it all! And this was by no means because my father did not love me: he thought the world of both me and my mother. That's just how it was, that was his character.

Worries, disappointments, failures tormented my poor father in the extreme: he became distrustful, irritable; often he was close to despair, he began to neglect his health, he caught cold and suddenly fell sick, he suffered for a short time and died such a quick and sudden death that for several days we were all beside ourselves from the shock. My mother was in a kind of numbed state; I was even afraid for her sanity. No sooner had my father died, than creditors began appearing from nowhere, in crowds they flooded in. We gave them whatever we had. Our little house on the Petersburg Side, bought by my father six months after our move to St Petersburg, was sold as well. I don't know how everything else was settled, but we ourselves were left without a roof over our heads, without shelter, without sustenance. My mother was suffering from a wasting disease, we were unable to feed ourselves, we had nothing to live on, ahead lay ruin. At that time I had just turned fourteen. And it was at this point that we were visited by Anna Fyodorovna. She keeps saying she is some sort of landowner, and is somehow related to us. My mother said she was related to us too, only very distantly. She had never visited us while my father was alive. She appeared with tears in her eyes and said she was very concerned for us; she commiserated with us on our loss, on our calamitous situation, and added that my father was himself to blame: that he had lived beyond his means, overstretched himself, and relied too much on his own powers. She revealed her desire to be on closer terms with us, suggested we forget things unpleasant for us all, and when my mother announced that she had never felt any hostility towards her, she became tearful, took my mother with her to church, and ordered a requiem service for the sweet man (that was how she referred to my father). After that she came to a solemn reconciliation with my mother.

Following lengthy introductions and forewarnings, Anna Fyodorovna painted in vivid colours our calamitous situation, orphanhood, hopelessness, helplessness, and invited us, as she herself expressed it, to find refuge with her. My mother thanked her, yet could not make up her mind for a long time; but since there was nothing for it, and it was quite impossible to arrange things in any other way, she finally did announce to Anna Fyodorovna that we gratefully accepted her proposition. I remember as if it were now the morning on which we moved from the Petersburg Side to Vasilyevsky Island. The morning was autumnal, bright, dry, frosty. My mother cried; I was dreadfully sad; my breast was bursting, my soul was wracked with some inexpressible, terrible anguish... It was a hard time.

. . . .

At first, while we, mother and I that is, had yet to settle into our new home, it was unpleasant somehow and strange living with Anna Fyodorovna. Anna Fyodorovna lived in her own house on the Sixth Line. In all there were five good rooms in the house. In three of them lived Anna Fyodorovna and my cousin Sasha, a child, an orphan without father or mother, whom she was bringing up. Then we lived in one room, and finally, in the last room next to ours was a poor student, Pokrovsky, Anna Fyodorovna's lodger. Anna Fyodorovna lived very well, more grandly than might have been supposed, but her status was a mystery, just as were her activities. She was always busy, always preoccupied, drove out or went out on foot several times a day, but what she did, with what she was occupied and why, that I could not guess at all. Her acquaintances were many and varied. Guests were always coming to visit her, and God knows who any of these people were, they always came on business of some sort and just for a minute. My mother always took me off to our room as soon as the bell rang. Anna Fyodorovna used to get dreadfully angry with mother about this and repeated constantly that we were just too proud, that we were proud beyond our powers, that we had nothing to be proud about, and she did not stop for hours on end. I did not then understand these reproaches about pride; in exactly the same way it is only now that I know, or at least presume to know, why my mother could not bring herself to live with Anna Fyodorovna. Anna Fyodorovna was a wicked woman; she tormented us constantly. Precisely why she invited us into her home is a mystery for me to this day. At first she was quite affectionate with us, and only later did she fully reveal her true character, when she saw that we were completely helpless and had nowhere to go. Subsequently she became extremely affectionate with me, even somehow crudely affectionate, to the point of flattery, but at first I too suffered along with my mother. She reproached us at every moment; she did nothing but talk about her benefaction. She introduced us to strangers as her poor relations, a helpless little widow and orphan, to whom out of charity, for the sake of Christian love, she had given refuge in her home. At the table her eyes followed every mouthful we took; but if we did not eat, the old story would begin again: we were disdainful, she would say; don't be so demanding, what I have is yours; we have nothing better ourselves. She criticised my father continually; she said he wanted to be better than other people, but it turned out badly; that he left his wife and daughter alone in the world, and if a benevolent relative had not turned up, a compassionate Christian soul, then God knows we might have been forced to starve to death in the middle of the street. The things she said! It was not so much bitter as repulsive to listen to her. My mother cried continually; her health became worse from day to day, she was visibly failing, yet at the same time we worked from morning till night, sewing to order, which did not please Anna Fyodorovna at all; she repeated continually that she did not keep a fashion house in her home. But we needed clothes, we needed to put something aside for unforeseen expenses, we needed to have our own money without fail. We saved up just in case, hoping that with time we would be able to move out somewhere. But my mother lost the last of her strength working: she grew weaker with every day. Sickness, like a worm, was visibly eating away at her life and bringing her closer to the grave. I saw it all, felt it all, suffered it all; it was all before my eyes!

The days passed, and each day resembled the one before. We lived quietly, as if we were not in the city at all. Anna Fyodorovna quietened down little by little as she herself became fully conscious of her power. In fact nobody ever thought of contradicting her. We in our room were separated from her quarters by a corridor, and alongside us, as I have already mentioned, lived Pokrovsky. He taught Sasha French and German, history, geography – all the sciences, as Anna Fyodorovna said, and in return received board and lodging from her. Sasha was a very bright girl, albeit playful and mischievous; she was then about thirteen. Anna Fyodorovna remarked to my mother that it would be no bad thing if I were to start studying too, since I had not finished the course at the boarding-school. My mother consented gladly, and for a whole year I was taught together with Sasha by Pokrovsky.

Pokrovsky was a poor, a very poor young man; his health did not permit him to go and study full time, and it was only out of habit that we called him a student. He lived modestly, meekly, and quietly, so you could not even hear him from our room. He was so strange in appearance; he walked so clumsily, bowed so clumsily, spoke so oddly, that at first I could not even look at him without laughing. Sasha played him up continually, especially when he was giving us lessons. And in addition he was by nature irritable, he was constantly getting angry, he would be beside himself over every little thing, he shouted at us, complained about us, and would frequently go off in a temper to his room without finishing the lesson. And he used to sit there for days on end over his books. He had a lot of them, and they were all such expensive, rare books. He taught somewhere else as well and received payment of some sort, so that no sooner did he get some money, than he would immediately go and buy himself some books.

With time I got to know him better, more intimately. He was the kindest, the worthiest man, the best of all I have had the good fortune to meet. My mother had great respect for him. Later on he was the best of friends to me too – after my mother, of course.

At first, although such a big girl, I joined with Sasha in her mischief, and we used to spend hours racking our brains over how we could tease him and make him lose his patience. He was dreadfully funny when he was angry and we found this extremely amusing. (I feel ashamed even remembering this.) Once we teased him about something almost to the point of tears, and I clearly heard him whisper: 'Wicked children.' I was suddenly embarrassed; I felt ashamed, and bitter, and sorry for him. I remember that I blushed to the roots of my hair, and all but had tears in my eyes as I started begging him not to be upset, and not to be offended by our silly mischief, but he closed his book, did not finish our lesson, and went off to his room. I was bursting with a sense of remorse the whole day. The idea that we children had reduced him to tears with our cruelty was unbearable for me. We must have been expecting his tears. Therefore we must have wanted them; we must have succeeded in exhausting the last of his patience; we must have forced him, the poor, unfortunate man, to recall his cruel destiny! I did not sleep at all that night in vexation, sorrow and remorse. They say that remorse eases the soul – on the contrary. I do not know how vanity came to be mixed in with my grief. I did not want him to think me a child. I was then already fifteen.

From that day on I began tormenting my imagination, creating thousands of plans of ways to make Pokrovsky suddenly change his opinion of me. But there were times when I was timid and shy; in my position then I could not decide upon anything, and restricted myself to dreams alone (and God knows what dreams!). I merely stopped joining Sasha in her mischief; he stopped getting angry with us; but that was not enough for my vanity.

Now I shall say a few words about the strangest, most curious and most pitiful man of any that I have ever happened to meet. I mention him now, precisely at this point in my notes, because right up until this period I had paid him almost no attention – then everything concerning Pokrovsky suddenly became of interest to me!

A little old man would sometimes appear in our house, dirty, badly dressed, small, grey-haired, awkward, clumsy, in short, as strange as could be. To look at him at first you might have thought he seemed ashamed of something, seemed to feel shameful about himself. For that reason he was always somehow hunched up, contorted somehow, and he writhed and grimaced so, you might have concluded, almost without error, that he was not in his right mind. He sometimes used to come and stand in our porch by the glass doors, not daring to enter the house. As soon as anyone went past – Sasha or I, or one of the servants that he knew to be more kindly towards him – he would immediately wave, beckon to the person, make various signs, and only when you nodded and called to him – the conventional sign that there were no strangers in the house and that he could go in whenever he liked – only then would the old man quietly open the door, smile joyfully, rubbing his hands in pleasure, and on tiptoe make straight for Pokrovsky's room. This was his father.

Later I learned this poor old man's story in detail. At one time he had been a civil servant somewhere, possessed not the slightest ability, and occupied the last, the most insignificant position at work. When his first wife died (the mother of Pokrovsky the student) he took it into his head to remarry, and he got married to a common sort. With the new wife in the house everything was turned upside down; she let nobody have a life of their own; she had everyone under her thumb. Pokrovsky the student was then still a child of about ten. His stepmother hated him. But fate smiled on the little Pokrovsky. Bykov, a landowner who knew

Pokrovsky the civil servant and had once been his benefactor, took the child under his protection and placed him in a school of some sort. And he took an interest in him because he knew his late mother, who, while still a girl, had had Anna Fyodorovna as a benefactress and had been given by her in marriage to Pokrovsky the civil servant. Mr Bykov, a friend and close acquaintance of Anna Fyodorovna, moved by generosity, gave the bride a dowry of five thousand roubles. Where this money went is unknown. That was the way Anna Fyodorovna told me all this; because Pokrovsky the student never liked talking about his family circumstances. His mother was said to have been very good-looking, and it seems strange to me that she made such a poor marriage with such an insignificant man… She died while still young, some four years after her marriage.

After school the young Pokrovsky went to some high school and then to the university. Mr Bykov, who came to St Petersburg very frequently, did not end his patronage here either. Because of his ill-health Pokrovsky was unable to continue his studies at the university. Mr Bykov introduced him to Anna Fyodorovna with his own recommendation, and in this way the young Pokrovsky was taken in, on condition that he teach Sasha anything that might be demanded.

Meanwhile the old man Pokrovsky, drowning his sorrows over his wife's cruelty, succumbed to the worst of vices and was almost always in a drunken state. His wife used to beat him, exiled him to the kitchen, and reduced him to such a condition that he finally grew accustomed to the blows and ill-treatment and did not complain. He was still a man of no great age, but as a result of his bad habits he had all but lost possession of his faculties. So the only sign of noble human feelings in him was his limitless love for his son. The young Pokrovsky was said to be the very image of his late mother. Was it not memories of his former kind wife that prompted such boundless love for him in the heart of the broken old man? The old man could not even talk of anything other than his son, and always visited him twice a week. He did not dare come more often because the young Pokrovsky could not bear his father's visits. Of all his faults, the first and most important was indisputably his disrespect for his father. Yet the old man was at times the most unbearable being in the world. Firstly, he was dreadfully curious, secondly, with his conversations and questions, which were the most pointless and senseless, he was continually preventing his son from working, and finally, he would sometimes appear in a drunken state. The son gradually broke the old man of his vices, of his curiosity and his continual chattering, and finally had his father obeying him in all things, as though he were an oracle, and not daring to open his mouth without permission.

The poor old man could not shower too much admiration and joy on his Petyenka, as he called his son. When he came to see him he almost always had a certain anxious and meek air, probably because of his uncertainty as to how his son would receive him, he generally spent a long time plucking up the courage to go in, and if I happened to be there, he used to spend twenty minutes or so questioning me – how was Petyenka, was he well, exactly what mood was he in, and was he busy with any important work? What exactly was he doing? Was he writing or busy thinking about something? When I had encouraged and reassured him sufficiently, the old man finally plucked up the courage to enter, and opened the door as quietly and cautiously as could be, at first poked just his head in, and if he saw that his son was not angry and gave him a nod, he slipped into the room, taking off his greatcoat and hat, which was constantly crumpled, full of holes and with a tattered brim, and hung everything up on a hook, did everything quietly, inaudibly; then he sat down cautiously on a chair somewhere and did not take his eyes off his son, tried to catch his every movement, wanting to guess his Petyenka's mood. If his son was a little out of sorts and the old man noticed it, he immediately rose from his seat and explained that 'you know, Petyenka, I just popped in, just for a minute. I've been a long way, you see, and I was passing by, and I dropped in for a rest.' And then without a word, humbly, he took his greatcoat and hat, and gradually opened the door again and left, forcing himself to smile, so as to contain the sorrow boiling up in his soul and not reveal it to his son.

But when the son received his father well, the old man was beside himself with joy. His pleasure showed in his face, in his gestures, in his movements. If his son began a conversation with him, he always raised himself a little from his seat and replied quietly, obsequiously, almost with awe, and always tried to use the most select, that is the most amusing expressions. But he did not have the gift of the gab; he always got confused and shy, so that he did not know what to do with his hands, what to do with himself, and afterwards he kept on whispering his reply to himself for a long time, as though wishing to correct himself. But if he succeeded in giving a good reply, the old man preened himself, straightened his waistcoat, tie and tailcoat and adopted an air of dignity. And sometimes he would be cheered and his courage built up to such an extent that he would quietly get up from his chair, go over to the bookshelf, take down some book or other and even read through something there and then, no matter what the book. All this he did with a look of feigned indifference and composure, as if he could do as he liked with his son's books at any time, as if his son's kindness was nothing new to him at all. But once I happened to see how the poor thing took fright when Pokrovsky asked him not to touch the books. He became confused, in his haste he put the book back upside down, then in trying to set things right he turned the spine to the rear, smiled, blushed, and did not know how to make amends for his crime. With his advice, Pokrovsky was gradually breaking his father of his bad habits, and as soon as he had seen him in a sober state two or three times running, the next time he visited he gave him in parting twenty-five or fifty kopeks or more. Sometimes he bought him a pair of boots, a tie or a waistcoat. And then the old man was proud as a peacock in his new things. Sometimes he would drop in on us. He brought Sasha and me gingerbread cockerels and apples, and spent the whole time talking to us about Petyenka. He asked us to study attentively, to be good, told us that Petyenka was a kind son, an exemplary son and, moreover, a learned son. Then he winked at us so funnily with his left eye, contorted himself so amusingly, that we could not stop ourselves from laughing and had a good chuckle at him. My mother was very fond of him. But the old man hated Anna Fyodorovna, although in front of her he was as quiet as a mouse.

I soon stopped studying with Pokrovsky. He continued to regard me as a child, a playful little girl on the same level as Sasha. This was very hurtful for me, because I tried with all my might to make amends for my earlier behaviour. But I went unnoticed. This irritated me more and more. I hardly ever spoke to Pokrovsky outside of lessons, indeed I was not able to speak. I would blush, become confused, and then cry in annoyance in a corner somewhere.

I do not know how all this would have ended, if a certain strange circumstance had not helped to bring us together. One evening when my mother was sitting with Anna Fyodorovna, I slipped into Pokrovsky's room. I knew he was out, and am not really sure why I took it into my head to go in there. Until then I had never even glanced into his room, although we had already been neighbours for over a year. On this occasion my heart was beating so hard, so hard, that it seemed to want to leap out of my breast. I looked all around with a particular curiosity. Pokrovsky's room was extremely poorly decorated; there was very little order. Five long bookshelves were nailed to the walls. Papers lay on the table and on the chairs. Books and papers! A strange idea came to me, and at the same time a certain unpleasant feeling of irritation took hold of me. It seemed to me that my friendship, my loving heart was not enough for him. He was educated, while I was stupid and knew nothing, had read nothing, not a single book... At this point I looked enviously at the long shelves, sagging under the weight of books. I was seized by annoyance, anguish, a kind of fury. I suddenly wanted to read his books, and I there and then resolved to do so, to the very last one, and as quickly as possible. I do not know, perhaps I thought that by learning everything that he knew I would be more worthy of his friendship. I rushed to the first shelf; without thinking, without pausing, I seized the first dusty old volume that came to hand, and, turning red, then white, trembling in agitation and fear, I carried the stolen book off to my room, bent on reading it in the night, by the nightlight, after my mother had fallen asleep.

But how annoyed I was when, on reaching our room, I hurried to open the book and saw some old, half-rotten Latin text, all eaten away by worms. I lost no time in going back. No sooner did I come to put the book on the shelf, than I heard a noise in the corridor and somebody's footsteps close by. I started to hurry and make haste, but the infuriating book had been so tightly packed in that when I had taken out the one, all the others had expanded of their own accord and closed ranks in such a way that now there was no more room left for their former comrade. I did not have the strength to squeeze the book in. However, I pushed the books as hard as I possibly could. The rusty nail on which the shelf was held, and which seemed to have been specially waiting for this moment to break, broke. One end of the shelf flew downwards. The books were scattered on the floor with a crash. The door opened and Pokrovsky entered the room.

It should be noted that he could not bear it when anybody took liberties in his domain. Woe betide anyone who dared touch his books! You can judge, then, my horror, when the books, large and small, in all possible formats, all possible sizes and thicknesses, plunged from the shelf, went flying, bounced under the table, under the chairs, all around the room. I might have tried to flee, but it was too late. 'It's over, I thought, it's over! I'm lost, done for! I play up and mess about like a ten-year-old child; I'm a stupid little girl! I'm a complete idiot!!' Pokrovsky was dreadfully angry. 'Well, that was all I needed!' he shouted. 'Well, aren't you ashamed of such bad behaviour!… Will you ever leave off?' And he rushed to pick the books up himself. I tried to bend down and help him. 'Don't bother, don't bother!' he shouted. 'You'd do better not to go places you haven't been asked.' But actually somewhat mollified by my submissive movement, he now continued more quietly, in his recent edifying tone, exploiting the rights of a recent teacher: 'Well, when are you going to grow up and get some sense? After all, just look at yourself, you're no longer a child, you know, you're not a little girl, you're already fifteen, after all!' And at this point, probably wanting to check if it was true that I was no longer little, he glanced at me and blushed to the roots of his hair. I did not understand; I stood before him and looked at him with my eyes wide open in amazement. He rose, came up to me with an air of embarrassment, got dreadfully confused, started to say something, seemed to be apologising for something, perhaps for having only now noticed that I was such a big girl. Finally I understood. I do not remember what happened to me then; I became confused, flustered, blushed even deeper than Pokrovsky, covered my face with my hands and ran out of the room.

I did not know what else I could do, where to go in my shame. The fact alone that he had caught me in his room! I could not look at him for three whole days. I blushed to the point of tears. The strangest ideas, funny ideas went round inside my head. One of them, the wildest, was

34

that I wanted to go to him, talk openly with him, confess everything to him, tell him everything candidly, and assure him that I had acted not like a silly little girl, but with good intentions. And I almost completely made up my mind to go, but, thank God, I did not have the courage. I can imagine what harm I would have done! Even now I feel ashamed recalling all this.

Several days later my mother suddenly fell dangerously ill. She did not get out of bed for two days, and then on the third night she was feverish and delirious. I had already stayed awake one night, caring for my mother, sitting at her bedside, bringing her drinks and giving her medicines at certain times. The next night I was completely worn out. I nodded off at times, there was a green mist in my eyes, my head was spinning, and I was ready to drop from exhaustion at any minute, but my mother's weak moans roused me, I started, woke up for a moment, and then drowsiness got the better of me again. I was in torment. I do not know, I cannot remember, but some terrible dream, some dreadful vision came into my disturbed mind in that agonising minute of struggle between sleep and wakefulness. I awoke in horror. The room was dark, the nightlight was going out, strips of light would suddenly flood the whole room, then flicker a little across the wall, then disappear entirely. For some reason I became frightened, a sort of horror came upon me; my imagination was stirred by the dreadful dream; anguish constricted my heart… I jumped up from the chair and some excruciating, terribly painful feeling made me shriek involuntarily. At that moment the door opened and Pokrovsky entered our room.

I remember only that I came round in his arms. He sat me down carefully in an armchair, handed me a glass of water and bombarded me with questions. I do not remember what answers I gave. 'You're ill, you're very ill yourself,' he said, taking me by the hand, 'you're in a fever, you're killing yourself, you're not sparing your own health; calm down, lie down and go to sleep. I'll wake you up in two hours, calm down a little… Lie down now, lie down!' he continued, not allowing me to utter a single word in objection. Tiredness had taken away the last of my strength; my eyes closed in weakness. I lay back in the armchair, meaning to fall asleep only for half an hour, and slept right through until morning. Pokrovsky woke me up only when the time came to give

35

my mother medicine.

The next day, at about eleven o'clock, when, after resting a little in the afternoon, I was preparing to sit in the armchair by my mother's bed once more with the firm resolve on this occasion not to fall asleep, Pokrovsky knocked at our room. I opened the door. 'It's boring for you sitting by yourself,' he said to me, 'here's a book for you; take it; it won't all be so boring.' I took it; I do not remember what book it was; I probably did not dip into it then, although I was awake all night. A strange inner agitation would not let me sleep; I could not keep still; several times I got up from the armchair and began walking around the room. Some inner contentment was flooding through the whole of my being. I was so glad of Pokrovsky's attention. I was proud of his anxiety and concern over me. I thought and dreamed the whole night through. Pokrovsky did not drop in again; and I knew he would not come and I looked forward to the next evening.

The following evening, when everyone in the house had already settled down, Pokrovsky opened his door and began talking to me, standing by the threshold of his room. I do not remember now a single word of what we then said to one another; I only remember that I was shy, confused, that I felt annoyed with myself and was impatient for the conversation to end, although I had myself desired it with all my might, had dreamed about it the whole day long, and had composed my questions and answers… From that evening there began the first strand of our friendship. Throughout the course of my mother's illness we spent several hours together every night. Little by little I overcame my diffidence, although after each of our conversations there was still something about which I could feel annoyance with myself. Yet with secret joy and proud pleasure I saw that he was forgetting his intolerable books because of me. By chance, jokingly, the conversation turned once to their falling from the shelf. That minute was strange, and I was somehow *too* frank and candid; ardour and a strange rapture carried me away, and I confessed everything to him… the fact that I wanted to study, to know something, that I was annoyed about being considered a little girl, a child… I repeat that I was in a very strange mood; my heart was tender, there were tears in my eyes, I concealed nothing and told him everything, everything – about my friendship for him, about my desire to love him, to be at one with him in the life of the heart, to comfort him, to soothe him. He looked at me strangely somehow, in embarrassment, in astonishment, and did not say a word to me. I suddenly felt dreadfully hurt, sad. It seemed to me that he did not understand me, that he was possibly laughing at me. I suddenly began to cry like a child, burst out sobbing, could not contain myself; it was as if I were having some sort of fit. He seized my hands, kissed them, pressed them to his chest, tried to talk me round, to comfort me; he was deeply touched; I do not remember what he said to me, but only that I cried, and laughed, and cried again, blushed, and could not utter a word in my joy. Yet despite my agitation I noticed that there nevertheless remained in Pokrovsky a certain embarrassment and constraint. He seemed unable to contain his wonder at my enthusiasm, my rapture, such sudden, ardent, fervent friendship. Perhaps at first he was just curious; subsequently his indecision vanished, and, with simple, direct emotion the same as my own, he accepted my attachment to him, my affable words, my attention, and replied to it all with the same attention, equally amicably and affably, as my sincere friend, as my own brother. My heart felt so warm, so well!... I did not hide or conceal anything; he saw all this, and with every day became more and more attached to me.

And I truly do not remember, was there anything he and I did not talk about in those agonising and at the same time sweet hours of our meetings, at night, in the flickering light of the lamp, and almost at the very bedside of my poor sick mother?... We talked about anything that came into our heads, that was torn from our hearts, that begged to be said – and we were almost happy... Oh, that was both a sad and a joyful time – all mixed together; and I feel both sad and joyful remembering it now. Memories, whether joyful or bitter, are always a torment; for me, at least; but even this torment is a delight. And when your heart begins to feel heavy, painful, weary, sad, then memories refresh and enliven it, as the dewdrops on a moist evening at the end of a hot day refresh and enliven a poor, sorry flower that has been burnt in the day's heat.

My mother was getting better, but I still continued to sit by her bed during the nights. Pokrovsky often gave me books; I read, at first so as not to fall asleep, then more attentively, then avidly; there suddenly opened up before me much that was new, previously unknown, unfamiliar to me. An abundant stream of new ideas, new impressions surged all at once towards my heart. And the greater the agitation, the greater the confusion and effort it cost me to accept the new impressions, the dearer they were to me, the more delightfully they rocked my entire soul. All at once, suddenly, they crowded into my heart, without allowing it any rest. A strange sort of chaos began to disturb the whole of my being. But this spiritual turbulence did not have the capacity or the power to upset me completely. I was too dreamy, and this saved me.

When my mother's illness was over, our meetings in the evenings and our long conversations ceased; we sometimes succeeded in exchanging a few words, often empty and insignificant, but it was a pleasure for me to give everything a significance of my own, a particular implicit value of my own. My life was full, I was happy, calmly, quietly happy. Thus passed several weeks…

One day old Pokrovsky called on us for some reason. He chatted to us for a long time, he was unusually cheerful, bright, talkative; he laughed, joked in his own way, and finally provided the solution to the riddle of his delight, announcing to us that in exactly one week it would be Petyenka's birthday, and that to mark the occasion he would visit his son without fail; that he would put on his new waistcoat, and that his wife had promised to buy him a pair of new boots. In short, the old man was entirely happy, and chatted about anything that entered his head.

His birthday! This birthday gave me no peace either by day or by night. I was absolutely determined to remind Pokrovsky of my friendship and give him something as a gift. But what? Finally I came up with the idea of giving him books. I knew that he wanted to have the complete works of Pushkin in the latest edition, and I decided to buy Pushkin for him. I had about thirty roubles of my own, earned by needlework. I had this money set aside for a new dress. I immediately sent our cook, old Matryona, to find out how much the complete Pushkin cost. Disaster! The price of all eleven books, adding in the cost of bindings, was at least some sixty roubles. Where could I find the money? I thought and thought, and did not know what decision to take. I did not want to ask my mother. Of course my mother would have certainly helped me; but then everyone in the house would have found out about our present; and in addition, this present would have turned into gratitude, payment for a whole year of Pokrovsky's labours. I wanted to give him a gift by myself, so that nobody else would know. While for his labours with me I wanted to be eternally indebted to him without any kind of repayment apart from my friendship. Finally I came up with an idea of how to get out of the predicament.

I knew that it was sometimes possible to buy a little-used, almost brand-new book from the second-hand booksellers in Gostiny Dvor[4] at half-price, if only you haggled. I resolved to make for Gostiny Dvor without fail. And so it came about; the very next day both we and Anna Fyodorovna turned out to need something. My mother was unwell, Anna Fyodorovna was feeling very conveniently lazy, so that I had to be entrusted with all the errands, and I set off together with Matryona.

To my delight, I found the Pushkin extremely quickly, and in an extremely attractive binding. I began haggling. At first I was asked for more than it cost in the shops; but then, albeit not without some difficulty, and after walking away several times, I got the merchant to the point where he had reduced the price and limited his demands to just ten silver roubles. What fun I had haggling!… Poor Matryona could not understand what was the matter with me and why I had taken it into my head to buy so many books. But it was dreadful! My entire capital consisted of thirty paper roubles, and the merchant simply would not agree to reduce the price. Finally I started imploring, I begged and begged and finally prevailed. He reduced the price, but only by two and a half roubles, and he swore that he was making this reduction only for my sake, I was such a nice young lady, and nothing would have made him do so for anybody else. Two and a half roubles short! I was ready to burst into tears in annoyance. But the most unexpected circumstance helped me in my misfortune.

Not far away, at another bookstall, I caught sight of old Pokrovsky. Crowding around him were four or five second-hand booksellers; they had him at his wit's end, they had muddled him completely. Each of them was offering him his wares, and the things they offered him, the things he wanted to buy! The poor old man stood in their midst, like some browbeaten creature, and did not know what he should take of what was on offer. I went up to him and asked what he was doing there.

The old man was very glad to see me; he loved me madly, perhaps no less than he did Petyenka. 'I'm here buying books, Varvara Alexeyevna,' he answered me, 'buying books for Petyenka. It'll be his birthday soon, and he likes books, so here I am buying them for him...' The old man always expressed himself oddly, and now, on top of everything, he was in the most dreadful confusion. No matter what he asked the price of, everything was a silver rouble, two, three silver roubles; he did not even ask the prices of the big books, but just looked at them enviously from time to time, fingered the pages, turned them in his hands and put them back in their places again. 'No, no, that's too dear,' he said in a low voice, 'but perhaps something from over here,' and at this point he began sorting through some slim little paperbacks, songbooks and almanacs; these were all very cheap. 'But why are you buying all this,' I asked him, 'this is all dreadful rubbish.' – 'Ah no,' he replied, 'no, you just have a look at what good books there are here; there are some very, very good books!' And he drawled out these last words so piteously, it seemed to me that he was ready to burst into tears in annoyance over why it was that good books were dear, and that at any moment a teardrop would drip from his pale cheeks onto his red nose. I asked whether he had much money. 'Well look,' and here the poor thing pulled out all his money, wrapped up in a grimy sheet of newspaper, 'here's a fifty-kopek piece, a twenty-kopek piece, and about twenty kopeks in copper.' Straight away I dragged him off to my bookseller. 'No fewer than eleven books here cost just thirty-two roubles fifty kopeks; I have thirty; add two roubles fifty kopeks, and we'll buy all these books and give him a present jointly.' The old man went mad with joy, spilled out all his money, and the bookseller loaded him up with the whole of our joint library. The little old man stuffed all his pockets with books, gathered them up in both hands, under his arms, and carried everything off home, giving me his word that the next day he would bring all the books quietly to me.

The next day the old man came to see his son, sat with him for an hour or so as usual, then dropped in on us and sat down beside me with the most comical air of secrecy. With a smile at first, rubbing his hands in proud pleasure at having some secret, he announced to me that the books had all been transferred to our house quite unnoticed and were standing in a corner of the kitchen under Matryona's protection. Then the conversation naturally moved on to the awaited celebration; then the old man became expansive on how we would present the gift, and the deeper he went into his subject and the more he spoke about it, the more noticeable it became to me that he had something on his mind about which he was unable, did not dare, was even afraid to express himself. I continued to wait in silence. The secret joy, the secret pleasure that I had easily read hitherto in his strange behaviour, his grimaces and his winking left eye, vanished. He was becoming ever more worried and anxious by the minute; finally he could not contain himself.

'Listen,' he began shyly, in a low voice, 'listen, Varvara Alexeyevna... do you know what, Varvara Alexeyevna?...' The old man was dreadfully embarrassed. 'You see: when his birthday arrives, you take ten books and give them to him yourself, from you, that is, on your part; and then I'll take one, the eleventh, and I'll give him a present from myself as well, personally, that is, on my part. So that, you see, you'll have something to give him and I'll have something to give him; we'll both have something to give him.' At this point the old man got confused and fell silent. I glanced at him; with shy expectation he was awaiting my sentence. 'But why is it you don't want to present them together, Zakhar Petrovich?' – 'Well, Varvara Alexeyevna, it's just that, the thing is... you know, I, it's, well...' – in a word, the old man became embarrassed, turned red, got stuck in his sentence and could not go on.

'You see, Varvara Alexeyevna,' he finally managed to say, 'I play up at times... That is, I want to inform you that I even keep on playing up almost, and play up all the time... I adhere to what is bad... That is, you know, it can get so cold out, and sometimes various unpleasant things occur as well, or you get to feel sad somehow, or something bad happens, and so at times I can't control myself and start playing up, and I sometimes have too much to drink. Petrusha doesn't like that at all. Then, you see, Varvara Alexeyevna, he gets cross, scolds me and recites various moral points to me. So that now I'd like to prove to him myself with my present that I'm changing for the better and beginning to behave myself properly; that I've saved up to buy him a book, saved up for a long time, because I hardly ever have any money at all, unless, as sometimes happens, Petrusha gives me some. He knows that.

Consequently, he'll see the use of my money and learn that I'm doing all this just for him.'

I felt dreadfully sorry for the old man. I did not think about it for long. The old man watched me anxiously. 'Well, listen, Zakhar Petrovich,' I said, 'you give him all of them!' – 'What do you mean, all? That is, all the books?...' – 'Of course, all the books.' – 'And from myself?' – 'From yourself.' – 'Just from myself? That is, in my name?' – 'Of course, in your name…' I seemed to be explaining it very clearly, but it was a long time before the old man understood.

'Of course,' he said pensively, 'yes! That'll be very good, that'd be extremely good, only what about you, Varvara Alexeyevna?' – 'Well, I won't give him anything.' – 'What do you mean?' cried the old man, almost in fright, 'so you won't give Petyenka any present, so you don't want to give him anything?' The old man took fright; at that moment he seemed ready to give up his proposition so that I too could give his son some gift. He was a kind old man! I assured him that I would be happy to give a present, only I did not want to deprive him of the pleasure. 'If your son is pleased,' I added, 'and you're happy, then I'll be happy too, because in secret, in my heart, I shall feel as if I'd actually given him a present.' The old man was completely reassured by this. He spent another two hours with us, but all that time he could not sit still, kept getting up, fussing about, making a noise, fooling around with Sasha, giving me surreptitious kisses, pinching my arms and pulling faces at Anna Fyodorovna on the sly. Anna Fyodorovna finally sent him packing from the house. In short, the old man let himself go in his delight to a degree that he had perhaps never done before.

On the great day he appeared at eleven o'clock precisely, straight from mass, in his tailcoat, respectably darned, and, indeed, wearing a new waistcoat and new boots. In each hand he held a bundle of books. We were then all sitting in Anna Fyodorovna's reception hall, drinking coffee (it was a Sunday). I think the old man began by saying that Pushkin was an extremely good poet; then, getting mixed up and confused, he moved on suddenly to say that one ought to behave well, and that if a man does not behave well, then that means he is playing up; that bad tendencies ruin and destroy a man; he even enumerated several ruinous examples of intemperance, and concluded by saying that for some time now he had been completely changed for the better and that his behaviour was now exemplary. That he had sensed the justice of his son's admonitions previously too, that he had sensed it all long ago and stored it all up in his heart, but now he had actually begun to control himself. In proof of which he was presenting books bought with money he had been saving up over a long period of time.

I could not contain my tears and laughter while listening to the poor old man; he knew how to lie, after all, when the need arose! The books were taken into Pokrovsky's room and put on a shelf. Pokrovsky guessed the truth at once. The old man was invited to lunch. That day we were all so cheerful. After lunch we played forfeits and cards; Sasha was playful and I did not lag behind. Pokrovsky was attentive to me and kept seeking an opportunity to have a talk with me in private, but I avoided it. That was the best day in four whole years of my life.

But now only sad and burdensome memories are to come; the story of my black days is to begin. Perhaps that is why my pen starts to move more slowly and seems to refuse to write any more. Perhaps that is why such enthusiasm and such love were there while I was going over in my memory the least details of my simple little life in the days when I was happy. Those days were so brief; they were replaced by grief, black grief that will end God alone knows when.

My misfortunes began with the illness and death of Pokrovsky.

He fell sick two months after the last events I described here. In those two months he was tireless in his efforts to find ways to make a living, for up until then he still had no proper position. Like all consumptives, he did not part with his hope for a very long life until his last moment. He had the chance of a place as a teacher somewhere, but that profession was repugnant to him. He could not serve anywhere in a government post because of ill-health. Moreover he would have had to wait a long time for the first instalment of his salary. In short, Pokrovsky saw nothing but failures everywhere; his character was getting worse. His health was deteriorating; he did not notice it. Autumn came on. Every day he went out in his light greatcoat to try and sort out his affairs, to plead and beg for a position somewhere – which tormented him inwardly; he got his feet wet, he got soaked in the rain, and finally he took to his bed, from which he rose no more... He died in the depths of autumn, at the end of October.

I hardly left his room throughout his illness, I looked after him and waited on him. Often I did not sleep for night after night. He was rarely conscious; he was often delirious; God knows what he spoke about: about his position, about his books, about me, about his father… and it was then that I heard much about his circumstances that I had not known before and about which I had not even guessed. In the early days of his illness everyone in the house looked at me strangely somehow; Anna Fyodorovna shook her head. But I looked everybody straight in the eye, and nobody thought of condemning me any more for my concern for Pokrovsky – not my mother, anyway.

Sometimes Pokrovsky recognised me, but that was rare. He was unconscious almost all the time. Sometimes he would be talking to somebody for ages and ages for nights on end in obscure, dark words, and his hoarse voice reverberated in his cramped room as if in a coffin; then I would feel afraid. Particularly on the last night he seemed to be in a frenzy; his suffering and anguish were awful; his groans tortured my soul. The whole house was in a sort of fright. Anna Fyodorovna kept praying for God to take him quickly. A doctor was called. The doctor said that the patient was sure to die before morning.

Old Pokrovsky spent the entire night in the corridor, right by the door to his son's room; some sort of bast matting was laid down for him there. He came into the room continually; he was dreadful to look at. He was so wracked with grief that he seemed completely devoid of feeling and sense. His head shook in fear. The whole of his body was trembling and he kept whispering something to himself, discussing something with himself. I thought he would go mad with grief.

Just before dawn, tired out by his spiritual pain, the old man fell asleep on his matting like a dead man. At seven o'clock his son was in the throes of death; I woke the father up. Pokrovsky was fully conscious and said goodbye to each of us. It was odd! I was unable to cry; yet my soul was being torn apart.

But I was tormented and tortured most of all by his last moments. Over a long period of time he kept on asking for something with his stiffening tongue, yet I could make nothing of his words. My heart was breaking from the pain! He was troubled for a whole hour, longing for something all the while, struggling to make some sign with his cold hands, and then he again began pleading piteously in his hoarse, hollow voice; but his words were just incoherent sounds, and again I could understand nothing. I brought everyone in the house to his bedside, offered him drinks; but he kept on sadly shaking his head. Finally I realised what he wanted. He was asking for the curtain at the window to be raised and the shutters to be opened. He doubtless wanted to look for the last time upon the day, upon God's earth, upon the sun. I pulled back the curtain; but the breaking day was sorrowful and sad, like the poor fading life of the dying man. There was no sun. Clouds spread across the sky in a misty shroud; it was so rainy, gloomy, sad. A light drizzle drummed against the window-panes and bathed them in streams of cold, dirty water; it was dull and dark. The rays of pale day barely struggled into the room and scarcely challenged the flickering light of the lamp that shone before the icon. The dying man looked at me ever so sadly and shook his head. A minute later he was dead.

Anna Fyodorovna herself made the arrangements for the funeral. The simplest of coffins was bought and a drayman hired. To cover the expenses Anna Fyodorovna seized all the books and all the belongings of the deceased. The old man argued with her, kicked up a row, took as many books as he could away from her, stuffed them into all his pockets, filled his hat and whatever else he could with them, fussed over them all three days, and did not even part with them when it was time to go to the church. All these days he seemed to be in a frenzy, in a daze, and with a strange sort of solicitude he kept bustling about beside the coffin: now he would be adjusting the wreath on the dead man, now lighting and removing candles. It was apparent that his thoughts could not rest properly on anything. Neither my mother nor Anna Fyodorovna was in the church for the funeral service. Mother was ill, while Anna Fyodorovna was almost completely set to go, but then had an argument with old Pokrovsky and stayed behind. Just I alone was there with the old man. During the service a sort of fear came over me, like a presentiment of the future. I was scarcely able to remain standing in the church. Finally the coffin was closed, the lid nailed down, it was put on the cart and off it went. I accompanied it only to the end of the street. The drayman drove at a trot. The old man ran behind him, and

sobbed out loud; running made his crying tremble and break. The poor thing dropped his hat and did not stop to pick it up. His head was wet from the rain; the wind was getting up; the frost whipped and stung his face. The old man did not seem to notice the bad weather and ran crying from one side of the cart to the other. The tails of his tattered frock-coat fluttered out in the wind like wings. Books poked out of all his pockets; there was some huge book in his arms to which he held on tight. Passers-by doffed their hats and crossed themselves. Some stopped to stare in wonder at the poor old man. Books were continually falling out of his pockets into the mud. People stopped him and pointed out his losses; he picked them up and set off once more in pursuit of the coffin. At the corner of the street some beggar woman joined with him to accompany the coffin. The cart finally turned the corner and disappeared from my sight. I went home. In dreadful anguish I threw myself upon my mother's breast. I squeezed her ever so tightly in my arms, kissing her and sobbing, pressing up against her fearfully, as though trying to keep my last friend in my embrace and not give her up to death... But death was already standing over my poor mother! ......
....

11TH JUNE

How grateful I am to you for yesterday's walk to the islands, Makar Alexeyevich! How nice and fresh it is there, what greenery there is there! It's so long since I saw any greenery; while I was ill, I kept on thinking I was going to die and that I was certain to die; judge then, what I should have been sensing yesterday, how I should have felt! You're not angry with me because I was so sad yesterday; I felt really well, really at ease, but at my very best moments I'm always sad for some reason. And the fact that I cried, that's nothing at all; I don't even know myself why I'm always crying. I feel things painfully, irritably; my impressions are morbid. The cloudless pale sky, the sunset, the hush of evening – all that, I just don't know, but somehow I was in the mood yesterday to respond seriously, distressfully to every impression, and so my heart was overflowing and my soul demanded tears. But why am I

46

writing all this to you? It's difficult for my heart to grasp all this, and to relate it is still more difficult. But perhaps you will even understand me. Both the sadness and the laughter! How kind you are, truly, Makar Alexeyevich! Yesterday you kept looking into my eyes to read in them what I was feeling, and you were enraptured by my delight. Whether it was a little shrub, a tree-lined path, a strip of water – you were sure to be there; always standing before me, preening yourself, and constantly gazing into my eyes, as if you were showing me your possessions. That proves you have a kind heart, Makar Alexeyevich. And that's why I love you. Well, goodbye. I'm ill again today; I got my foot wet yesterday and as a result caught a cold; Fedora has got something wrong with her too, so we're both sick now. Don't forget me, come and visit often.

Your

V. D.

12TH JUNE

My sweet Varvara Alexeyevna!
And there was I thinking, my dear, that you'd describe all yesterday's doings to me in real poetry, but just one simple little sheet was all you managed. What I'm saying is that although you didn't write me very much on your little sheet, still on the other hand you wrote it unusually well and sweetly. Both the nature, and various rural scenes, and all the rest about feelings – in short, you described all that very well. Whereas me now, I've got no talent. Scribble ten pages if you want, nothing comes of it at all, you can't describe a thing. I've tried. You write to me, my dear, that I'm a kind, forgiving person, incapable of harming my neighbour, and who comprehends the Lord's bounty, manifested in nature, and, finally, you offer me various other words of praise. All this is true, my dear, all this is absolutely true; I really am the way you say, I know it myself; but when you read the things you write, your heart is touched, like it or not, and then various distressing ideas occur. But just listen to me, my dear, I'll tell you something.

I'll begin with the fact that I was just seventeen years old when I went into the service, and now my service career will already soon be hitting thirty. Well, it can't be denied, I've worn out my share of uniforms; I've matured, become wiser, seen a lot of people; I've spent some time, I can say that I've spent some time in the world, so that once they even wanted to put me forward for a medal. Perhaps you don't believe it, but truly, I'm not lying to you. So then, my dear, wicked people turned up to do all this! But I can tell you, my dear, that even if I am an ignorant man, a stupid man, maybe, still my heart is the same as anyone else's. So do you know, Varenka, what a wicked person did to me? But it's shameful to say what he did; you might ask – why did he do it? Just because I'm meek, just because I'm quiet, just because I'm kind! I wasn't to their liking, and so they started on me. At the beginning it began with them saying, 'Well, don't bother asking Makar Alexeyevich'. And now they've finished up with, 'Well, of course it's Makar Alexeyevich!' There, my dear, you see how it all progressed: everything onto Makar Alexeyevich; all they could do was make Makar Alexeyevich proverbial throughout our department. And it wasn't enough to make me proverbial and all but a term of abuse – they've had a go at my boots, my tunic, my hair, my figure: nothing suits them, everything needs to be changed! And you know, all this is repeated from time immemorial every day God sends. I'm used to it, because I get used to everything, because I'm a meek man, because I'm a little man; but, however, what's the reason for all this? What have I done wrong to anyone? Have I stolen anybody's rank or anything? Have I blackened anybody in front of our superiors? Asked for somebody else's bonus? Cooked up some plot or something? It'd be a sin even to think such a thing, my dear! How could I do all that? Just have a look and see, my dear, do I have enough capacity for cunning and ambition? So what's the reason then for such misfortunes to fall upon me, God forgive me? After all, you find me a worthy man, and you're incomparably better than all of them, my dear. After all, what is the greatest civic virtue? Yevstafy Ivanovich remarked the other day in a private conversation that the most important civic virtue is knowing how to coin it in. He said this as a little joke (I know it was a joke), yet the moral is that you shouldn't be a burden on anyone; but I'm not a burden on anyone! I have my own crust of bread; true, it's a simple crust of bread, at times it's even stale; but it's there, earned by my labours, exerted lawfully and irreproachably. Well what's to be done? After all, I know myself that I'm not doing much in copying things out; but all the same I'm proud of it: I work, I sweat. Well, and what's actually so bad about my copying things? What, is it a sin to copy things or something? 'He copies things!' they say. 'This bureaucratic rat,' they say, 'copies things!' Well, what's so dishonourable in that? My writing's so clear and nice, it's a pleasure to look at, and His Excellency is satisfied; I copy out the most important documents for him. Well, I have no style, after all, I know myself that I haven't got any, curse it; that's the very reason I've not been a success at work, and here I am now even writing to you, my dear, any old how, without any embellishments and as the thoughts come into my heart… I know all this; but if everyone started composing things, however, who then would think of copying? That's the question I'm posing, and I'm asking you to reply to it, my dear. Well, so I do now recognise that I'm needed, that I'm essential, and that there's no reason to put somebody off with nonsense. Well, maybe I am a rat, if they've found a resemblance! But this rat is needed, and the rat is useful, and people hold on to this rat, and this rat is getting a bonus – that's the kind of rat it is! Still, that's enough about this topic, my dear; after all, I didn't even want to talk about it, but I got a bit carried away. All the same, it's nice from time to time to do justice to yourself. Goodbye my dear, sweetheart, my kind little comforter! I'll visit, I'll be sure to visit you, I'll see how you are, my little flower. But don't you be miserable in the meantime. I'll bring you a book. Well, goodbye then, Varenka.

Your sincere well-wisher

Makar Devushkin

20TH JUNE

Dear Sir, Makar Alexeyevich!

I'm writing to you quickly, I'm in a hurry, I'm finishing a job to a deadline. The thing is, you see, there's a good buy to be had. Fedora says that some acquaintance of hers is selling a uniform, quite nice and new, underclothes, a waistcoat and cap, and, so they say, it's all very cheap; so you should buy it. After all, you're not in any need now and you have some money; you say yourself you do. That's enough, please, don't be mean; for it's all necessary. Just look at yourself, what old clothes you go around in. It's shameful! Patched all over. And you don't have anything new; I know it, even though you assure me that you have. God alone knows what you did with it. So do as I say and buy it please. Do it for me; if you love me, buy it.

You sent me some linen as a present; but listen, Makar Alexeyevich, you're spending all your money, you know. It's no joke, the amount you've spent on me – it's an awful lot of money! Ah, how you do love squandering it! I don't need it; it was all completely unnecessary. I know, I'm certain that you love me; truly, it's not necessary to remind me of this with presents; and it's hard for me to accept them from you; I know what they cost you. Once and for all – that's enough; do you hear? I beg you, I implore you. You ask me, Makar Alexeyevich, to send you the continuation of my notebook; you want me to finish it. I don't know how I even managed to write what I've written! But I won't have the strength now to talk about my past; I don't even want to think about it; these memories frighten me. And talking about my poor mother, who left her poor child as prey for those monsters, is most difficult of all. My heart bleeds at the memory alone. All this is still so fresh; I've not had the time to make sense of it, let alone calm down, although it's all more than a year ago now. But you know everything.

I told you about Anna Fyodorovna's current ideas; she keeps accusing me of ingratitude and rejects every accusation that she is in association with Mr Bykov! She invites me to go back to her; she says I'm a beggar and that I've taken the wrong path. She says that if I return to her, she takes it upon herself to set the whole business with Mr Bykov to rights and she'll force him to make amends for his blameworthiness before me. She says that Mr Bykov wants to give me a dowry. Who cares about them! I'm well enough here with you, with my kind Fedora, who with her attachment to me reminds me of my late nanny. You may be only my distant relation, yet you defend me with your name. Whereas I don't know them; I shall forget them if I can. What else do they want from me? Fedora says it's all gossip, that in the end they'll leave me alone. God grant it be so!

V. D.

My dear, my little sweetie!

I want to write, but I don't even know where to begin. I mean, how very strange it is, my dear, that you and I now live like this. What I'm saying is that I never spent my days in such happiness. Well, it's just as if the Lord had blessed me with a little house and family. My dearest little child, just what is this you're saying about the four shirts I sent you? After all, you did need them – I found out from Fedora. And for me, my dear, it's a particular joy to please you; so it's my pleasure, so you leave me alone, my dear; leave me be and don't contradict me. Nothing of the sort ever happened to me, my dear. I've entered the world now, you see. Firstly, I'm living doubly, because you also live very close to me too, and to my delight; and secondly, I was invited to tea today by a lodger, my neighbour Ratazyayev, that same civil servant who has literary evenings. There's a gathering today; we're going to read some literature. That's the way we are now, my dear – there you are! Well, goodbye. I've written all this, you know, without any apparent purpose, and solely to inform you of my good fortune. You've let it be known through Tereza, darling, that you need some coloured silk for embroidery; I'll buy it, my dear, I'll buy it, I'll buy some silk too. And tomorrow I'll have the enjoyment of giving you complete satisfaction. I even know where to buy it. And I myself now remain

    Your sincere friend

Makar Devushkin

Madam, Varvara Alexeyevna!

I am informing you, my dear, that ever such a pitiful occurrence has taken place in our apartment, truly, truly worthy of pity! Before five o'clock in the morning today Gorshkov's little one died. I don't know what of, though, maybe some sort of scarlet fever or something, the Lord knows! I paid the Gorshkovs a visit. Well, my dear, how poor their room is! And what disorder! And it's not surprising: the whole family lives in one room, just divided up with screens for the sake of decency. They already have a little coffin in there – a simple, but quite nice little coffin; they bought it ready made, the boy was about nine; they say he was shaping up well. But it's pitiful looking at them, Varenka! The mother doesn't cry, but she's so sad, the poor woman. Things may even be easier for them, with one off their shoulders already; but they still have two left, a babe in arms and a little girl, she'll be about six or so. What a pleasant thing, indeed, to see: here's a child suffering, your own child what's more, and there's not even anything just to help him! His father sits in his old, soiled tailcoat on a broken chair. His tears flow, and perhaps not even in grief, but just out of habit, there's a discharge from his eyes. He's so peculiar! He's always blushing when you start talking to him, he gets confused and doesn't know how to reply. The little girl, the daughter, stands leaning up against the coffin, and the poor little thing is so dismal and pensive! And I don't like it, my dear, Varenka, when a child gets pensive; it's not nice to look at! Some sort of rag doll lies on the floor beside her – she doesn't play; she holds her finger on her lips; stands there, not moving. The landlady gave her a sweet; she took it, but didn't eat it. It's sad, Varenka, isn't it?

Makar Devushkin

25TH JUNE

Kindest Makar Alexeyevich! I'm sending you back your book. It's the most worthless, horrid little book! You shouldn't even have picked it up. Where did you dig up such a gem? Joking aside, surely you don't like such books, Makar Alexeyevich? I've been promised that in a few days something will be found for me to read. I'll share it with you too, if you like. But goodbye for now. Truly, there's no time to write any more.

V. D.

26TH JUNE

Dear Varenka! The fact is that I didn't actually read that horrid little book, my dear. True, I read a little bit, I can see that it's whimsy, just written merely for the sake of making you laugh, to amuse people; well, I think, it really ought to be entertaining; Varenka will probably like it too; and I went and sent it to you.

But now Ratazyayev has promised to give me something truly literary to read, well, then you'll have some books, my dear. That Ratazyayev knows his stuff, he's a real buff; he writes himself, and boy, how he writes! Such a lively pen and masses of style; in pretty much every word, that is, there's something, in the emptiest, in just the most ordinary, common word, so that even I could sometimes say to Faldoni or Tereza – look, even there he's got style. I go to his evenings too. We smoke tobacco and he reads to us, he reads for five hours or so, and we keep listening. It's lovely grub, not literature! It's such a delight – flowers, simply flowers; make a bouquet out of every page! He's so courteous, kind, affectionate. Well what am I to him, well what? Nothing. He's a man with a reputation, and what am I? I simply don't exist; but he's well-disposed even to me. I copy some things out for him. Only don't you think, Varenka, that there's some fiddle here, and that it's precisely because of the fact that I do copying for him that he's well-disposed towards me. Don't you go believing gossip, my dear, don't you go believing base gossip! No, I do it from the heart, of my own free will, for his pleasure, and the fact that he's well-disposed towards me, well it's he that's like that for my pleasure. I understand the delicacy of the deed, my dear. He's a kind, a very kind man and an incomparable writer.

And it's a good thing, Varenka, literature, a very good thing; I learned that from them a couple of days ago. A profound thing! A thing that strengthens people's hearts, instructs, and – various other things about all this are written in this book of theirs. It's very well written! Literature is a picture, that is in a certain way a picture and a mirror; the expression of passion, a kind of subtle criticism, an exhortation to edification and a document. I picked all this up from them. I'll tell you frankly, my dear, that you sit amongst them, you know, you listen (and like them too you smoke a pipe as well, if you want), but when they start to compete and argue about various matters, then at this point I simply pass, at this point, my dear, you and I will have to pass, pure and simple. At this point I simply turn out to be a complete idiot, I'm ashamed of myself, so that the whole evening you're looking out for a way to get so much as half a word into the general topic, but that very half word, as if on purpose, isn't even there! And you feel sorry, Varenka, about yourself, that you're just not up to it; that, as the saying goes, you've been better fed than taught. After all, what do I do now in my spare time? I sleep like an utter fool. Whereas instead of unnecessary sleeping, I could get on with something that was pleasant too; such as sitting down and doing a bit of writing. It's both useful for you and good for others. I mean, my dear, you just take a look at how much they earn, may the Lord forgive them! There's Ratazyayev even – how he earns! What is it to him to write a sheet? Why, on some days he's even written five, and he says he earns three hundred roubles a sheet. Some little anecdote or other, or something curious – five hundred, pay up, like it or not, just pay up! If not – then we put as much as a thousand in our pockets next time! What about that, Varvara Alexeyevna? That's not all! He has a little notebook of poems, and the poems are all kind of small – seven thousand, my dear, he asks seven thousand, just think. I mean, that's a land holding, that's property capital! He says they try to give him five thousand, but he doesn't take it. I reason with him, saying 'take the five thousand from them, old chap, and then be done with them – after all, five thousand is real money!' No, he says, they'll give seven, the villains. He really is so full of tricks!

So then, my dear, if that's the way it's gone, so be it, I'll copy out for you a bit from *Italian Passions*. That's the name of his composition. Just read this then, Varenka, and judge for yourself:

'…Vladimir shuddered, and passions began to bubble up violently within him, and his blood boiled…

'"Countess," he cried, "Countess! Do you know how terrible is this passion, how boundless this madness? No, my dreams did not deceive me! I am in love, rapturously, violently, madly in love! All your husband's blood cannot quench the mad, bubbling rapture of my soul! Trifling obstacles cannot check the all-destructive fire of Hell that harrows my exhausted breast. Oh Zinaida, Zinaida!…"

'"Vladimir!" whispered the countess, beside herself, inclining towards his shoulder…

54

'"Zinaida!" cried the enraptured Smelsky.

'A sigh was exhaled from his breast. The fire flared up with a bright flame on the altar of love and harrowed the breasts of the unfortunate sufferers.

'"Vladimir!…" whispered the countess in ecstasy. Her breast rose, her cheeks were crimson, her eyes burned…

'A new, dreadful marriage was concluded! . . . .

. . . .

'Half an hour later the old count entered his wife's boudoir.

'"Well then, darling, should we not order the samovar to be prepared for our dear guest?" he said, giving his wife's cheek a tweak.'

There you are. I ask you, my dear, after that – well, how do you find it? True, it's a little racy, there's no question about that, but then it is good. How good it is, it's so good. And then allow me to copy out for you another little fragment from the tale *Yermak and Zyuleika*.

Imagine, my dear, that the Cossack Yermak, the wild and terrible conqueror of Siberia, is in love with Zyuleika, daughter of the ruler of Siberia, Kuchum, and whom he has taken captive. An event straight out of the age of Ivan the Terrible, as you can see. Here's a conversation between Yermak and Zyuleika:

'"You love me, Zyuleika! Oh say it again, say it again!…"

'"I love you, Yermak," whispered Zyuleika.

'"Heaven and earth, I thank you! I am happy!… You have given me everything, everything to which my agitated soul has aspired since the years of my adolescence. So this is where you were leading me, my guiding star; so this is why you led me here, beyond the Stone Girdle! I shall display my Zyuleika to the whole world, and man, those violent monsters, will not dare to blame me! Oh, if these secret sufferings of her tender soul are comprehensible to them, if they are capable of seeing an entire epic poem in my Zyuleika's one tear-drop! Oh let me wipe away this tear-drop with kisses, let me drink it, this heavenly tear-drop… unearthly one!"

'"Yermak," said Zyuleika, "the world is wicked, men are unjust. They will persecute us, they will condemn us, my sweet Yermak! What will a poor maiden who has grown up in her father's yurt amidst her native Siberian snows do in your cold, icy, soulless, vain world? Men will not understand me, my beloved, my love!"

'"Then a whistling Cossack sabre will be raised on high above them!" cried Yermak, his eyes wandering wildly.'

And what about Yermak now, Varenka, when he finds out his Zyuleika has had her throat cut. The blind elder, Kuchum, using the darkness of the night and in the absence of Yermak, has slipped into his tent and cut his daughter's throat, wanting to deliver a mortal blow to Yermak, who has deprived him of his sceptre and crown.

'"Does it give me pleasure to strike iron against stone?" shouted Yermak in a wild frenzy, whetting his knife of damask steel on the shaman's stone. "I must have their blood, blood! They must be hewn, hewn, hewn!!!"'

And after all this Yermak, with no strength to live without his Zyuleika, throws himself into the River Irtysh, and that's how it all ends.

Well and what about this, for example, just a little fragment in a comically descriptive mode, written strictly to make you laugh:

'"Do you know Ivan Prokofyevich Zheltopuz?[5] Well, the same one that bit Prokofy Ivanovich's leg. Ivan Prokofyevich is a man of difficult character, but at the same time of rare virtues; but on the other hand Prokofy Ivanovich is extremely fond of radishes with honey. And when Pelageya Antonovna was still acquainted with them… But do you know Pelageya Antonovna? Well, the same one that always puts her skirt on inside out."'

I mean, it's just hilarious, Varenka, simply hilarious! We were rolling around laughing while he was reading us that. What a man, may the Lord forgive him! Anyway, my dear, it may be a bit whimsical, and certainly too playful, but at the same time it's innocent, without the slightest hint of free thinking or liberal ideas. It should be noted, my dear, that Ratazyayev is of excellent conduct and is for that reason a superb writer, unlike other writers.

And indeed, I mean, sometimes you do get an idea come into your head… well then, if I wrote something, well what would happen then? Well then, for example, let's suppose that suddenly, without warning, a book appeared under the title *The Poems of Makar Devushkin*! Well what would you say then, my little angel? How would you look on, what would you think of that? And I'll tell you for my own part, my dear, that when that book of mine appeared, I'd definitely not dare to show myself on Nevsky Avenue then. I mean, what would it be like when everyone could say that 'here comes the composer of literature and poet, Devushkin', that 'that really is Devushkin himself'! Well what would I begin to do then, for example, with my boots? I'll remark to you in passing, my dear, that they're almost always patched, and what's more the soles, to tell the truth, are coming away at times most improperly. Well what would happen then, when everyone found out that Devushkin the writer has patched boots! Some *contesse-duchesse* or other would find out, well what would she say, the dear? Perhaps she wouldn't even notice; for I assume that *contesses* have nothing to do with boots, let alone a clerk's boots, (because, after all, there are boots and boots), but she'd be told about everything, my own friends would give me away. Ratazyayev there would be the first to give me away; he pays calls on Countess V.; he says he's always there, he visits her informally too. He says she's such a dear, she's a literary sort of lady, he says. He's a scallywag, that Ratazyayev!

But that's enough on that topic anyway; I'm writing all this, my little angel, you know, just for fun, to entertain you. Goodbye, sweetheart! I've scribbled down a lot for you here, but that's actually because I'm in the most cheerful frame of mind today. We all had lunch together today with Ratazyayev, and (they're so naughty, my dear!) they passed around such a sweet wine… well, why should I be writing to you about that! You just be sure you don't invent anything about me, Varenka. I mean, all this means nothing. I'll send some books, I'll be sure to send. A work by Paul de Kock[6] is being passed around here, only you won't be getting any Paul de Kock, my dear… No, no! Paul de Kock isn't suitable for you. What they say about him, my dear, is that he makes all the St Petersburg critics nobly indignant. I'm sending you a pound of sweets – I bought them specially for you. Eat them up, my poppet, and think of me with every sweet. Only don't you chew the fruit-drops, just suck on them, or else your little teeth will start aching. But perhaps you like candied peel too? You write and tell me. Well, goodbye then, goodbye. May the Lord be with you, sweetheart. And I shall remain

Your most faithful friend

Makar Devushkin

27TH JUNE

Dear Sir, Makar Alexeyevich!

Fedora says that if I wish it, some people will be glad to take an interest in my situation and obtain for me a very good post as a governess in a certain house. What do you think, my friend – should I go or not? Of course, I shan't be a burden on you then, and the post seems to be a well-paid one; but on the other hand, it's horrible somehow to go into an unfamiliar household. They're landowners of some sort. They'll start finding things out about me, they'll begin asking questions, being curious – well, what will I say then? What's more, I'm so unsociable, so wild; I like to feel at home in a corner I'm used to and stay for a long time. It's better somehow in a place you're accustomed to: you may not have an easy life, but it's better all the same. And moving in with them what's more; and then God knows what the work will be like; perhaps they'll just make you nurse the children. And there's the people too; they're already changing their third governess in two years. Do advise me, Makar Alexeyevich, for God's sake, should I go or not? And why is it you never come to visit me in person? You just look in from time to time. On Sundays at mass is almost the only time we see each other. What an unsociable person you are! You're just like me! And after all, I am almost your relative. You don't love me, Makar Alexeyevich, and sometimes I'm very sad by myself. There are times, especially in the twilight, you're sitting there all on your own, Fedora goes off somewhere. You sit thinking and thinking – you remember all the old things, both the joyous and the sad – it all passes before your eyes, it's all glimpsed as if out of a mist. Familiar faces appear (I'm beginning to see them almost for real) – most often of all I see my mother... And what dreams I have! I feel my health is ruined; I'm so weak; I had a bad turn today too, when I was getting out of bed in the morning, and on top of that I've got such a bad cough! I feel, I know that I shall die soon. And who will bury me? And who will follow my coffin? And who will feel sorry for me?... And so perhaps I shall be obliged to die in a strange place, in a strange house, in a strange corner!... My God, what a sad life, Makar Alexeyevich! Why is it, my friend, you keep on feeding me sweets? I truly don't know where it is you get so much money from. Ah my friend, look after your money, for God's sake look after it. Fedora is selling the rug I embroidered; they're giving fifty paper roubles. That's very good: I thought it would be less. I'll give Fedora three silver roubles and I'll sew myself a dress, just a nice simple one, but a warm one. I'll make you a waistcoat, I'll make it myself and I'll choose some good material.

Fedora got a book for me – *The Tales of Belkin*, which I'm sending you, in case you want to read it. Only please don't get it dirty and don't keep it too long; it's somebody else's book; it's a work by Pushkin. Two years ago my mother and I read these tales together, and now it was so sad for me rereading them. If you have any books then send them to me – but only in the event that you've received them from someone other than Ratazyayev. He'll probably give you something of his own composition, if he's had anything printed. How is it that you like his works, Makar Alexeyevich? Such nonsense... Well, goodbye! How I've chattered away! When I'm sad, I'm glad to chatter about anything at all. It's a medicine: you feel better straight away, and especially if you express everything that's in your heart. Goodbye, goodbye, my friend!

Your

V. D.

My dear, Varvara Alexeyevna!

Enough of this grieving! You really should be ashamed of yourself! Come now, my little angel; how is it you get such ideas? You're not ill, poppet, not ill at all; you're blooming, truly blooming; a little pale, but blooming all the same. And what are these dreams and visions you're having? You should be ashamed, my dear, come now; just you spit on these dreams, simply spit. Why is it I sleep well? Why is it there's nothing wrong with me? You take a look at me, my dear. I live my life, sleep peacefully, I'm fit as a fiddle, fresh as a daisy, it's a pleasure to see. Come now, come now, poppet, you should be ashamed. Pull yourself together. I mean, I know that little head of yours, my dear, no sooner has it come across anything than you've started dreaming and grieving about something. Stop it for my sake, dear. Become a servant? Never! No, no, no! And whatever are you thinking of, what's come over you? And moving out, what's more! Oh no, my dear, I won't allow it, I take up arms with all my strength against such an intention. I'll sell my old tailcoat and walk the streets in nothing but my shirt, but we're simply not going to have you in need. No, Varenka, no. I know you! It's fancy, pure fancy! But what's for sure is that Fedora alone is to blame for everything: she's clearly a silly woman and has put all this into your head. But don't you trust her, my dear. And I don't suppose you know everything yet, sweetheart?… She's a silly woman, shrewish and cantankerous; she hounded her late husband to his grave too. Or she probably made you angry somehow. No, no, my dear, not for anything! And what will happen to me then, what will remain for me to do? No, Varenka, sweetheart, you put it out of your little head. What do you lack here with us? We take delight in you, you love us – so go on living quietly over there, do sewing or read, or perhaps don't do the sewing – it's all the same, only stay with us. Otherwise, you judge for yourself, well what will it be like then?… I'll get you some books, and then perhaps we'll get together again to go for a walk somewhere. Only come now, my dear, come now, you must be sensible and not fill your head with nonsense! I'll come and see you, and in a very short time, only in return you accept my direct and frank admission: it's wrong, sweetheart, very wrong! Of course I'm not an educated man and I know myself that I'm not educated, that I had a poor boy's schooling, but that's not what I want to talk about, it's not me that's the point here, but I'll stand up for Ratazyayev, if you don't mind. He's my friend, and for that reason I'll stand up for him. He writes well, he writes very, very, and once again, very well. I don't agree with you, and can't agree with you at all. It's written colourfully, sharply, with figures, there are various ideas; it's very good! Perhaps you were reading without feeling, Varenka, or you were in a bad mood when you were reading, you were angry with Fedora about something, or something bad had happened to you. No, you just read it with feeling, a bit better, when you're happy and cheerful and you're in a good frame of mind, like, for example, when you've got a sweet in your mouth – read it then. I don't argue (who could be against it?), there are writers still better than Ratazyayev, there are even those still much better, but both they are good and Ratazyayev is good; they write well and he writes well. He does his bit of writing and he does it alright, and he does a very good thing in doing a bit of writing. Well goodbye, my dear; I can't write any more; I need to hurry, I've got something to do. See to it, my dear, my precious little flower, keep calm, and may the Lord remain with you, while I remain

Your faithful friend

Makar Devushkin

PS Thank you for the book, my dear, we'll read Pushkin too; but today I'll definitely come and see you in the evening.

1ST JULY

My dear Makar Alexeyevich!

No, my friend, no, it's no life for me amongst you. I've changed my mind and find that I'm very wrong to refuse such a well-paid post. There I'll at least be sure of a crust of bread anyway; I'll try hard, I'll earn the affection of strangers, I'll even try to change my character if needs be. Of course it's painful and hard living among strangers, looking for charity from strangers, hiding yourself away and constraining yourself, but God will help me. I can't just remain unsociable for ever. I've already had similar experiences. I remember when I was still small and used to go to the boarding-school. The whole of Sunday you'd be playing and jumping about at home, sometimes my mother would even scold – but all was well, all was good in your heart and bright in your soul. Evening would start to approach, and a deathly sadness would take hold, you had to go to the boarding-school at nine o'clock, and everything there was strange, cold and strict, the governesses were so bad-tempered on Mondays, it was as if your spirit was being squeezed, you felt like crying; you'd go into a corner and have a little cry all on your own, hiding the tears in case you were called lazy; but I wasn't even crying about having to study at all. Well then? I got used to it, and then later on, when I was leaving the boarding-school, I cried as well, saying goodbye to my friends. And I'm doing wrong, being a burden on both of you. This idea is torment for me. I'm telling you all this frankly because I'm used to being frank with you. Don't I see how Fedora gets up ever so early every day and gets on with her washing and works late into the night? And old bones like some rest. Don't I see that all your money is going on me, you're putting your last kopek on the table and spending it on me? Not with your fortune, my friend! You write that you'll sell your last possession, but you won't leave me in need. I believe it, my friend, I believe in your kind heart – but it's now that you speak like this. Now you have some unexpected money, you've received a bonus; but later on what will happen, later on? You know yourself – I'm always ill; I can't work the way you do, although I would be only too glad, and there isn't always work to be had. So what remains for me? To be torn apart in anguish looking at the two of you, both so kind. How can I be of even the least use to you? And why am I so essential to you, my friend? What good have I done you? I am simply attached to you with all my soul, I love you very much, deeply, with all my heart, but – bitter is my fate! – I know how to love and can love, and that's all, but not do good, not repay you for your good deeds. Don't keep me then any longer, have a think and tell me your final opinion. In expectation I remain

Your loving

V. D.

Whimsy, whimsy, Varenka, simply whimsy! Leave you like that, and like that you might think anything over with that little head of yours. This isn't right and that isn't right! And I can see now that it's all whimsy. What is it you lack with us then, my dear, just tell me that! You're loved, you love us, we're all contented and happy – what else is there? Well, and what are you going to do among strangers? I mean, you probably don't yet know what a stranger is?... No, you be so good as to ask me about it, and I'll tell you what a stranger is. I know him, my dear, I know him well; I've had occasion to eat his bread. He's angry, Varenka, angry, so very angry that if your little heart is wanting, he tears it apart with a complaint, a reproach and a nasty look. You're nice and warm with us – as if you'd found refuge in a little nest. What's more, you'll leave us headless, in a way, too. Well, what will we do without you; what will I, an old man, do then? We don't need you? You're of no use? In what way, of no use? No, my dear, you judge for yourself, how can you be no use? You're of great use to me, Varenka. You have this beneficial influence... Here I am thinking of you now, and I'm cheerful... I write you a letter sometimes and set out all my feelings in it, to which I receive a detailed reply from you. I've bought you a bit of a wardrobe, had a hat made; at times you send me some errand and I... No, how can you be no use? And then what am I going to do alone in my old age, what will I be good for? Perhaps you didn't even think of that, Varenka; no, you think precisely of that – 'what, then, what will he be good for without me then?' I've grown used to you, my dear. Or else what will come of it? I'll go down to the River Neva, and that'll be the end of it. Yes, it's the truth, it'll be like that, Varenka; what else will remain for me to do without you? Ah, sweetheart, Varenka! Clearly you want a drayman to cart me away to the Volkovo cemetery; some common old beggar woman alone to accompany my coffin, you want them to scatter sand on top of me, then go away and leave me there alone. It's a sin, a sin, my dear! Truly, it's a sin, I swear to God, it's a sin! I'm sending you back your book, my little friend, Varenka, and if, my little friend, you ask my opinion regarding your book, then I shall say that in all my life I've not had occasion to read such splendid books. I ask myself now, my dear, how is it that I've lived like such an oaf before, may the Lord forgive me? What was I doing? What forests have I come from? I mean, I know nothing, my dear, I know precisely nothing! I know nothing at all! I'll tell you straight, Varenka – I'm not an educated man; until now I've read little, I've read very little, almost nothing: I've read *A Picture of a Man*, a wise composition; I've read *The Boy Who Plays Various Things on the Bells* and *The Cranes of Ibycus* – that's all, and I've never read anything more. Now I've read *The Stationmaster* here in your book; you know, what I'll say to you, my dear, is that sometimes it happens that you're alive, but you don't know that right alongside you there you've got this book, where the whole of your life is laid out in detail. And things that never occurred to you yourself previously, well here, as you begin to read in this book, bit by bit you yourself both remember, and discover and guess the meaning of. And finally, this is also why I came to love your book: another work, such as it is, you read and read till you're fit to burst sometimes – and it's so complicated that it's as if you don't even understand it. I, for example, I'm dim, I'm dim by nature, so I can't read works that are too important; but you read this – it's like I wrote it myself, it's as if, to give an example, my own heart, such as it is, he took it, turned it inside out for people and described everything in detail – that's what! And it's a simple matter, my God; nothing to it! Truly, I would have written it the same way too; why shouldn't I have written it? After all, I feel the same too, just absolutely like in the book, and I too have at times been in such situations myself as, to give an example, this Samson Vyrin, the poor man. And how many Samson Vyrins are there among us, just such warm-hearted, hapless men! And how cleverly everything is described! I almost shed tears, my dear, when I read that he'd turned to drink, the sinner, so that he'd lost his senses, become a drunkard and slept the whole day under a sheepskin coat, and drowned his sorrows with grog, and cried piteously, wiping his eyes with his dirty coat-flap, when he remembered his lost sheep, his daughter Dunyasha! No, it's like real life! You read it; it's like real life! It lives! I've seen it myself – all this lives near me; there's Tereza, if you like – why go further afield? – there's our poor civil servant too, if you like – after all, perhaps he's just as much a Samson Vyrin, only he has a different name, *Gorshkov*. It's a common business, my dear, and it could happen to you and to me. And the count that lives on Nevsky Avenue or the embankment, he too will be the same, he'll just seem to be different, because they have everything their own way, in the very best tone, but he too will be the same, anything could happen, and the same thing could happen to me too. That's the way it is, my dear, and here you are wanting to leave us too; but, you know, Varenka, sin could take me unawares. And you could ruin both yourself and me, my dear. Ah, you little flower of mine, for God's sake turn all these free thoughts out of your little head and don't torment me for no reason. Well how are you, my weak, unfledged little nestling, how are you to feed yourself, to keep yourself from ruin, to defend yourself from villains? Come now, Varenka, pull yourself together; don't listen to nonsensical advice and slanders, but read your book again, read it attentively; it'll be of benefit to you.

I talked to Ratazyayev about *The Stationmaster*. He told me that it's all old hat and that books now all have pictures and various descriptions; now I didn't really take in very well what it was he was saying there. He concluded that Pushkin is good and that he brought glory to Holy Russia, and he told me a lot of other things about him. Yes, it's very good, Varenka, it's very good; you read the book again attentively, follow my advice and make me, an old man, happy by your obedience. Then the Lord Himself will reward you, my dear, He'll be sure to reward you.

Your sincere friend

Makar Devushkin

6TH JULY

Dear Sir, Makar Alexeyevich!
Fedora brought me fifteen silver roubles today. How glad she was, the poor thing, when I gave her three silver roubles! I'm writing to you in haste. I'm cutting you a waistcoat now – the material's lovely – yellow with little flowers. I'm sending you a book; it's all different stories in it; I've read some of them; read one of them under the title *The Greatcoat*. You're trying to persuade me to go to the theatre with you; won't that be expensive? Only if it's somewhere in the gallery. I've not been to the

theatre for ever such a long time now, truly, I don't even remember when it was. Only again I'm still afraid that this plan will cost a lot. Fedora only shakes her head. She says you've started living completely beyond your means; and I can see that for myself; how much you've spent on me alone! See that nothing bad should come of it, my friend. As it is, Fedora has been telling me about some rumours – that it seems you've had an argument with your landlady about not paying her some money; I'm very afraid for you. Well, goodbye; I'm in a hurry. I've got a little job to do; I'm changing the ribbons on my hat.

V. D.

PS Do you know, if we go to the theatre, then I'll put on my new hat and wear my black mantilla on my shoulders. Will that look nice?

7TH JULY

Dear Madam, Varvara Alexeyevna!

… So then, I'm still talking about yesterday's business. Yes, my dear, we were struck by whimsy too in days of old. I fell for this little actress, fell head over heels, yet that would still have been alright; but the oddest thing was the fact that I hardly saw her at all, went to the theatre just once, and despite all that, I fell for her. At that time about five young people of the very excitable kind were living right next door to me. I fell in with them, like it or not I fell in, although I always kept within the bounds of decency in relation to them. Well, so as not to be left out, I myself even agreed with them about everything. They talked a lot to me about this actress! Every evening, as soon as the theatre's on, the whole company – they never had two coins to rub together for any essentials – the whole company set out for the theatre, to the gallery, and they just clap and clap and call and call for this actress – they just go crazy! And then they won't let you go to sleep; they're talking about her the whole night long, each one calls her 'his Glasha', they're all in love with her alone, they all have the same songbird in their hearts. They got defenceless little me excited as well; I was still a youngster then. I don't know myself how I came to be at the theatre with them, in the fourth tier, in the gallery. As far as seeing goes, I could see only the edge of the curtain, but on the other hand I could hear everything. The little actress really did have a pretty little voice – ringing, like a nightingale, honeyed! We all clapped till our hands were dropping off, we shouted and shouted – in short, we all but had to be dealt with, and one of us did get led out, it's true. I arrived home – it was as if I was walking around drunk! Only one silver rouble was left in my pocket, and it was a good ten days till pay-day. So what would you think, my dear? The next day, before going to work, I dropped in to a French perfumer's, spent all my capital buying some scent or other and some nice-smelling soap from him – I don't even know myself why I bought all this then. And I didn't have dinner at home, but kept on walking past her windows. She lived on Nevsky Avenue on the third floor. I went home, rested there for an hour or so, and went back to Nevsky again, just so as to walk past her windows. I went about like that for a month and a half, running after her; I was continually hiring smart cabs and kept on going up and down past her windows; I got myself absolutely tired out, got into debt, and then I fell out of love with her too; I got fed up with it! So that's what an actress is capable of doing to a decent man, my dear! But anyway, I was a youngster, a youngster then!…

M. D.

My dear Madam, Varvara Alexeyevna!
Your book, received by me on the sixth of this month, I hasten to return to you and at the same time hasten in this my letter to have things out with you. It's a bad thing, my dear, a bad thing that you've reduced me to such an extremity. Allow me, my dear: every condition is determined by the Almighty to the lot of man. It is determined that one is to wear a general's epaulettes, another to be a titular counsellor in the civil service; this one is to command, and this one to obey, uncomplaining and in fear. It is already calculated according to a man's capability; one man is capable of one thing, and another of another thing, and the capabilities are arranged by God Himself. I've been in the service for

thirty years now; I work irreproachably, am of sober conduct, have never been detected in disorderly behaviour. As a citizen, with my own consciousness I consider myself to have my shortcomings, but at the same time my virtues too. I'm respected by my superiors, and His Excellency himself is satisfied with me; and although he has to this day not yet given me any particular signs of favour, still I know that he is satisfied. I've lived long enough to turn grey; I don't know of any great sins on my part. Of course, who isn't at fault in little things? Everyone's at fault, and even you are at fault, my dear! But I've never been detected in major misdeeds or misdemeanours, doing something or other against regulations or in breach of public order, I've never been detected in that, it hasn't happened; a medal was even on its way – well what of it! All this in conscience you ought to have known, my dear, and he ought to have known it; if he took it upon himself to give a description, then he ought to have known everything. No, I didn't expect this from you, my dear; no, Varenka! I didn't expect such a thing, particularly from you.

What! So after this you can't even live your life quietly in your little corner – whatever it might be like – live without muddying any water, as the saying goes, bothering nobody, knowing the fear of God and yourself, in such a way that you aren't bothered either, so that no one forces their way into your kennel to spy on you and say: 'how do you manage there in the domestic line, have you got, for example, a nice waistcoat, is the underwear that you ought to have to be found; do you have boots and how are they soled; what do you eat, what do you drink, what do you copy?'... And what's so wrong with the fact, my dear, that perhaps I do sometimes go on tiptoe where the roadway isn't so good, the fact that I look after my boots! Why write about another person that he's sometimes in need, that he doesn't drink tea? And it's as if everybody really ought to drink tea then without fail! And do I look into everyone's mouths saying 'what's that he's chewing?' Who is it I've upset like that? No, my dear, why upset other people when they don't bother you! Well and here's an example for you, Varvara Alexeyevna, this is what it means: you're working away, earnestly, diligently – right! – and your superiors themselves respect you (whatever the case, still they respect you all the same) – and then right under your very nose, for no apparent reason, without any warning, somebody gives you a real roasting. Of course, it's true, at times you have something new made for yourself – you're glad, you don't sleep, you're so glad, you put on new boots, for example, so sensuously – it's true, I've felt that, because it's nice seeing your leg in such a smart boot – that's accurately described! But all the same, I'm genuinely surprised at how Fyodor Fyodorovich let such a book pass without attention and didn't stand up for himself. It's true that he's still a young dignitary and likes to do a bit of shouting occasionally; but why not do a bit of shouting? And why not give someone a roasting too, if the likes of us need a roasting? Well let's suppose it's like this, for example, roasting someone for the sake of tone – well it can be done for the sake of tone too; training's needed; a warning needs giving; because – and this is between you and me, Varenka – the likes of us won't do anything without a warning, we all try just to be on a list somewhere, so as to say 'I do such and such a job', but they avoid work all the time. And as there are multiple ranks, and each rank demands to be roasted in absolute accordance with rank, it's natural that after that the tone of roasting turns out multiranking too – it's in the order of things! And you know, that's what holds society together, my dear, the fact that we all set the tone for one another, that we all give one another a roasting. Without this precaution society couldn't hold together and there'd be no order. I'm genuinely surprised at how Fyodor Fyodorovich let such an insult pass without attention!

And what's such a thing written for? And what's it necessary for? So will one of the readers have a greatcoat made for me as a result of this, or something? Will he buy me new boots, or something? No, Varenka, he'll read it through and then demand a sequel. You hide sometimes, you hide, you conceal yourself inside whatever you've got, you're afraid at times to poke your nose out – anywhere at all, because you tremble in the face of gossip, because out of everything that could be found on earth, out of everything they'll make you a satire, and then the whole of your civic and family life goes around in literature, everything is printed, read, mocked, gossiped about! And then you won't even be able to show yourself in the street; I mean, it's all so well demonstrated here, that now you can recognise the likes of us just by the way we walk. Well, it would have been alright if towards the end he had at least improved, toned things down, included something, for example, even after the point where they scattered paper on his head, such as 'despite all this he was a virtuous and good citizen, did not deserve such treatment from his colleagues, did the bidding of his superiors (here some example could be given), wished nobody any harm, believed in God and was mourned when he died' (if he really must have him die). But best of all would be not to leave him to die, the poor thing, but make it so that his greatcoat was found, so that the general, learning in greater detail of his virtues, asked to have him transferred to his own office, promoted him and gave him a good salary, so you can see how it would be: evil would be punished and virtue would triumph, and his colleagues in the office would all be left with nothing. I, for example, would have done it like that; for otherwise, what's he got here that's so special, what's he got here that's so good? It's just some trivial example from mundane, nasty, everyday life. And how did you come to make up your mind to send me such a book, my dear? I mean, it's an ill-intentioned book, Varenka; it's simply unrealistic, because it couldn't be the case that such a clerk existed. And I mean, after something like that you've got to make a complaint, Varenka, a formal complaint.

Your most humble servant

Makar Devushkin

27TH JULY

Dear Sir, Makar Alexeyevich!
The latest events and your letters frightened me, astonished me and threw me into bewilderment, but Fedora's accounts have made everything clear to me. Yet why did you have to despair so and fall into the sort of abyss into which you have fallen, Makar Alexeyevich? Your explanations didn't satisfy me at all. You see, was I not right when insisting on taking that well-paid post I was offered? What's more, my latest incident really does frighten me too. You say your love for me

forced you to hold back from me. Even when you were claiming that you were spending on me only money you had in reserve, money which, as you said, you had in the bank in case of need, even then I could already see that I owed you a great deal. But now that I've learned that you had no money at all, that after finding out by chance about my needy situation and being touched by it, you made up your mind to spend your salary, which you took in advance, and sold even your clothes when I was ill – now I'm put in such an agonising position by this discovery, that I still don't know how to take all this and what to think about it. Ah, Makar Alexeyevich! You should have stopped at your first good deeds, to which you were inspired by compassion and kindred feelings, and not wasted money subsequently on unnecessary things. You've betrayed our friendship, Makar Alexeyevich, because you haven't been open with me, and now, when I see that all you had has gone on smart clothes, on sweets, on outings, on the theatre and books for me – I'm now paying dear for it all in regret over my unforgivable thoughtlessness (for I accepted everything from you without worrying about you yourself); and everything with which you wanted to give me pleasure has now turned to woe for me and left in its wake only useless regret. I've noticed your anguish recently, and although I've been anxiously expecting something myself, still what has happened now did not even occur to me. What! Could you have lost heart to such a degree already, Makar Alexeyevich? But what will everyone who knows you think of you now, what will they say about you now? You, whom I and everybody else respected for kindness of spirit, modesty and good sense, you have now suddenly fallen into such a repulsive vice, in which, apparently, you've never been detected before. What happened to me when Fedora told me you'd been found in the street in a drunken state and brought to the apartment accompanied by the police! I was rooted to the ground in astonishment, even though I was expecting something unusual, because you'd been missing for four days. But have you thought, Makar Alexeyevich, about what your superiors will say when they learn the true reason for your absence? You say that everyone laughs at you; that everyone has found out about the bond between us, and that your neighbours refer to me too in their mockery. Pay no attention to it, Makar Alexeyevich, and for God's sake calm down. I'm also frightened by your incident with these officers, I've heard about it vaguely. Explain to me, what does it all mean? You write that you were afraid of being open with me, afraid of losing my friendship through your confession, that you were in despair, not knowing how to help in my sickness, that you sold everything in order to support me and keep me out of hospital, that you got into debt as deep as you could and have problems with your landlady every day – yet concealing all this from me, you chose the worse path. And now I've found out everything after all. You were embarrassed about making me admit that I was the reason for your unfortunate position, yet now you've brought twice as much woe upon me with your behaviour. All this has amazed me, Makar Alexeyevich. Ah, my friend, misfortune is an infectious disease. The poor and unfortunate should avoid one another, so as not to become even more infected. I've brought misfortunes upon you such as you'd not suffered before in your modest and secluded life. All this is torturing and killing me.

Write to me frankly now about everything that's happened to you and how you resolved to do such a thing. Calm me, if you can. It isn't vanity that makes me write now about my calm, but my friendship and love for you, which nothing can erase from my heart. Goodbye. I await your reply with impatience. You thought badly of me, Makar Alexeyevich.

Your sincerely loving

Varvara Dobroselova

28TH JULY

My priceless Varvara Alexeyevna!
Well then, as everything is over now and everything is little by little returning to its former state, this then is what I'll say to you, my dear: you're worried about what people will think of me, to which I make haste to announce to you, Varvara Alexeyevna, that my pride is dearer to me than anything. In consequence of which, and in reporting to you about my misfortunes and all these disturbances, I can inform you that

none of my superiors knows anything yet, and won't know either, so they'll all feel respect for me as previously. I'm afraid of one thing: I'm afraid of gossip. Our landlady shouts, but now that with the help of your ten roubles I've paid off a part of my debt to her, she only grumbles and no more. As far as the others are concerned, they're alright as well; you just don't need to ask to borrow money from them, because otherwise they're alright as well. And in conclusion to my explanations I'll tell you, my dear, that I hold your respect for me above anything in the world, and I console myself with this now during my temporary disturbances. Thank God that the first shock and the first unpleasantness are over and you took it in such a way that you don't consider me a treacherous friend and egoist because, lacking the strength to part with you and loving you as my little angel, I kept you near me and deceived you. I've set about my work zealously now and started carrying out my duties well. Yevstafy Ivanovich didn't even say a word when I passed him yesterday. I won't conceal from you, my dear, that my debts and the poor state of my wardrobe are killing me, but again that's nothing, and regarding that too, I beseech you, don't despair, my dear. You send me another fifty-kopek piece, Varenka, and this fifty-kopek piece pierced my heart for me. So that's the way it's become now, so that's how it is! That is, it's not I, an old fool, that's helping you, a little angel, but you, my poor little orphan, helping me! Fedora did well, getting some money. I have no hope for the moment, my dear, of receiving any, but if any hopes revive a little, I'll write off to you about it in detail. Yet gossip, gossip worries me most of all. Goodbye, my little angel. I kiss your little hand and beg you to get well. The reason I'm not writing in detail is that I'm hurrying to work, for by my diligence and zeal I want to make up for all my faults and omissions in my duties; I'm putting off the continuation of the narrative about all the occurrences and about the incident with the officers until the evening.

Your respectful and your sincerely loving

Makar Devushkin

Ah, Varenka, Varenka! It's just precisely now that the fault is on your side and will remain on your conscience. You knocked the last bit of sense out of me with your letter, perplexed me, and it's only now, when I've delved into the depths of my heart at leisure, that I've seen that I was right, I was absolutely right. I'm not talking about my shindy (forget it, my dear, forget it), but about the fact that I love you and that it wasn't at all unwise for me to love you, not at all unwise. You don't know anything, my dear; but if you only knew why it all is, why it is that I should love you, then you'd have said something else. You're just saying all this reasonable stuff, but I'm sure that in your heart there's something else entirely.

My dear, I don't even know myself and don't remember very well everything that happened between me and the officers. You should note, my little angel, that until that time I was in the most dreadful confusion. Imagine that for a whole month already I had, so to speak, been holding on by a single thread. The situation was most calamitous. I was hiding from you, and at home as well, but my landlady made a real song and dance. I didn't mind that. Let the worthless old woman shout, but one thing was that it was shameful, and the second was the fact that, the Lord knows how, she'd found out about the bond between us and shouted such things about it so that the whole house could hear, that I was dumbstruck and I blocked up my ears too. But the point is that others didn't block up their ears, on the contrary, they pricked them up. Even now, my dear, I don't know what to do with myself…

And so, my little angel, it was all this, all this motley collection of various disasters that finally did for me. All of a sudden I hear strange things from Fedora, that an unworthy suitor has come to your house and insulted you with an unworthy proposal; that he's insulted you, deeply insulted you, I judge by myself, my dear, because I too am deeply insulted myself. It was at this point, my little angel, that I went off my head, at this point that I lost control and was completely done for. Varenka, my friend, I ran out in some unheard-of frenzy, and I wanted to go and see him, the sinner; I didn't even know what I wanted to do, because I don't want you, my little angel, to be hurt! Well, I felt sad!

And at the time there was rain, and slush and terrible anguish!... I was already on the point of wanting to return... And it was then that I fell, my dear. I met Yemelya, Yemelyan Ilyich, he's a clerk, that is he was a clerk, but now he's no longer a clerk, because he was sacked from our office. I don't even know what he does now, how he manages; well, so we went off together. Then – well what is it to you, Varenka, well is it fun or something to read about your friend's misfortunes, his calamities and the story of the temptations he's undergone? On the third day, in the evening – it was Yemelya that put me up to it – I went to see him, the officer. I asked our yardman about the address. If the truth be known, my dear, I'd been keeping an eye on this fine fellow for a long time; I'd trailed him, even when he was still quartered in our house. Now I can see that what I did wasn't proper, because I wasn't myself when I was announced to him. To tell the truth, Varenka, I don't even remember anything; I only remember that there were a great many officers with him, or else I was seeing double – God knows. I don't remember what I said either, only I know that I said a lot in my noble indignation. Well it was at this point that I was ejected, at this point that I was thrown down the stairs, that is it wasn't as if I was completely thrown down, but just, you know, pushed out. You already know, Varenka, how I returned; that's all there is to it. Of course I've let myself down and my pride has suffered, but, I mean, no outsiders know about that, nobody knows except you; well and in that case it's just the same as if it hadn't even happened. Perhaps that's how it is, Varenka, what do you think? The only thing I know for sure is the fact that last year our Aksenty Osipovich made an attack on the person of Pyotr Petrovich in just the same way, but in secret, he did it in secret. He enticed him into the porter's room, I saw all this through a gap in the door; and when there he dealt with things as was necessary, but in a noble way, because nobody saw it apart from me; well and I'm alright, that is I mean to say that I didn't announce it to anyone. Well and since then Aksenty Osipovich and Pyotr Petrovich are alright. Pyotr Petrovich is the proud type, you know, so he didn't tell anyone, and so now they both bow and shake hands. I'm not arguing, Varenka, I don't dare argue with you, I've fallen a long way and, what is more dreadful than anything, I'm a loser in my own opinion, but that was probably written in my stars, that's probably my fate – and you can't escape from your fate, you know that yourself. Well, there's a detailed explanation of my misfortunes and calamities, Varenka, there you have it – everything such that it's better left unread, still at the same time… I'm a little unwell, my dear, and I've lost all my playful feelings. For which reason, bearing witness to you of my attachment, love and respect, I now remain, Varvara Alexeyevna, my dear madam,

Your most humble servant

Makar Devushkin

29TH JULY

Dear Sir, Makar Alexeyevich!
I read both your letters and was left open-mouthed! Listen, my friend, either you're keeping something from me and have written to me only a part of all your problems, or… truly, Makar Alexeyevich, your letters still have the ring of some sort of distress… Come and see me, for God's sake, come today; and listen, you know what, just come straight to us for dinner. I simply don't know how you're getting on there and how you've come to terms with your landlady. You don't write anything about any of that and it's as if you're keeping something back on purpose. So goodbye, my friend; be sure to visit us today; and you'd do better if you always came to us for dinner, Fedora is a very good cook. Farewell.

Your

Varvara Dobroselova

1ST AUGUST

My dear, Varvara Alexeyevna!
You're pleased, my dear, that God has sent you in your turn the chance to repay kindness with kindness and to show your gratitude to me. I believe this, Varenka, and I believe in the goodness of your angelic heart, and I'm not saying this to you to chide – only don't reproach me like you did that time with having squandered everything in my old age. Well, I

was at fault that way, what's to be done, if you really think there has to be some blame; only it costs me a lot to hear such a thing from you, my little friend. But don't you get angry with me for saying this; there's an aching all through my breast, my dear. Poor people are capricious – that's the way nature arranges it. I felt that even before, and now I've felt it still more. The poor man, he's demanding, he even sees God's world differently and looks askance at every passer-by, and he casts a troubled gaze around him, and he listens carefully to every word, as if wondering 'are they saying something about me over there?'. Such as 'why is he so unattractive? What exactly would he be feeling? How, for example, would he look from this side, how would he look from that side?' And everyone, Varenka, is aware that the poor man is worse than a bit of old rag and can't get any respect from anyone, whatever they might write – them, those scribblers, whatever they might write! Everything about the poor man will be just as it used to be. And why is it that it will be just as it was before? Because the poor man, in their opinion, ought to have everything inside out; he should have nothing at all that's sacred, say pride of some sort, oh no! Yemelya there was saying the other day that he had a subscription set up for him somewhere, so that for every ten-kopek piece he had a sort of official inspection made of him. People thought they were giving him their ten-kopek pieces for nothing – but no, they were paying to be shown a poor man. Nowadays, my dear, even good deeds are done in an odd way somehow… but perhaps they were always done like that, who knows? Either they don't know how to do them, or else they're real experts – one or the other. Perhaps you didn't know this, well, there you are! We're no good at anything else, but we're famous for this! And how does the poor man know all this and think all this sort of stuff? How? Well, from experience! And because he knows, for example, that just round the corner there's this gentleman that goes to a restaurant somewhere and says to himself – 'what's that pauper of a clerk going to be eating today? Well I'm going to have sauté papillot, while perhaps he'll be having porridge without any butter'. And what business is it of his that I'm going to have porridge without any butter? Such a person can be found, Varenka, he can, that thinks of nothing but such things. And they go around, those indecent satirists, looking to see whether you put the whole of your foot down on a stone or just tread

77

on tiptoes; then it's such and such a clerk, from such and such a department, a titular counsellor, has his bare toes poking out of his boot, and his elbows have got holes in them' – and then they go and describe all this, and such rubbish gets printed… And what business is it of yours that my elbows have got holes in them? Well, and if you'll forgive me a coarse word, Varenka, then I'll tell you that the poor man has the same shame on this account as you have, to give an example, maidenly shame. I mean, you wouldn't think of – forgive my coarse word – disrobing in front of everyone; and in exactly the same way the poor man doesn't like people looking into his kennel either and asking 'what will his family relations be like?' – you see. So why did you have to offend me, Varenka, siding with my enemies, encroaching on the honour and pride of an honest man!

Yes and I was sitting in the office today like such a baby bear-cub, such a plucked sparrow, that I almost burnt up in shame for myself. I felt ashamed, Varenka! It's quite natural to be timid when your bare elbows are showing through your clothes and your buttons are dangling on threads. And as if on purpose, I had all this in such disorder! Like it or not, your spirits fall. Why, Stepan Karlovich himself began talking about work with me today, he talked and talked, and then as if by chance he added: 'Oh my good fellow, Makar Alexeyevich!' – but he didn't finish saying what he was thinking, only I'd already guessed it all myself and blushed so that even my bald patch turned red. It's alright really, but all the same it's upsetting, makes you think seriously about things. Has something been found out? May God forbid that, well, anything should be found out! I confess I have suspicions, strong suspicions about one man. I mean, it's nothing to these villains! They'll betray you! They'll betray the whole of your private life for nothing at all; they hold nothing sacred.

I know now whose doing it is: it's Ratazyayev's doing. He's acquainted with someone in our department, and, you know, in between conversations he probably passed everything on with additions; or perhaps he told the story in his own department, and it crawled out into our department. And in our apartment everybody knows everything down to the last detail, and people point at your window; I know for sure they point. And when I set off yesterday to have dinner with you, they all leaned out of the windows, and the landlady said 'the devil's got mixed up with a baby' and then she called you by an indecent name. But all this is nothing in the face of Ratazyayev's vile intention to put you and me in his writing and to describe us in a subtle satire; he said this himself, and good people from our apartment passed it on to me. I simply can't even think about anything, my dear, and I don't know what I should decide on. It can't be denied, we've angered the Lord God, my little angel! You wanted to send me some book, my dear, to fend off boredom. Forget it, my dear, the book! What is it, a book? It's an invented story with characters! A novel is rubbish and it's written for rubbish, just for idle people to read; believe me, my dear, believe my many years of experience. And what if they go on and on to you about some Shakespeare or other, with 'you see, literature has Shakespeare' – well Shakespeare's rubbish too, it's all utter rubbish, and it's all done just to satirise!

Your

Makar Devushkin

2ND AUGUST

Dear Sir, Makar Alexeyevich!

Don't worry about anything; if the Lord God wills it, everything will turn out well. Fedora got a pile of work both for herself and for me, and we set about it most cheerfully; perhaps we'll put everything to rights. She suspects that all my latest problems are not unknown to Anna Fyodorovna; but it's all the same to me now. Somehow I'm unusually cheerful today. You want to borrow money – may the Lord preserve you! There'll be countless woes later on, when it has to be repaid. Better live more closely with us, visit us more often and pay no attention to your landlady. So far as your other enemies and ill-wishers are concerned, I'm sure you're tormenting yourself with futile doubts, Makar Alexeyevich! Look out, you know I told you last time that your style is extremely uneven. Well, goodbye, farewell. I expect you here without fail.

Your

V. D.

My little angel, Varvara Alexeyevna!

I hasten to inform you, O light of my life, that I've had certain hopes revived. But allow me, my little girl – you write, my little angel, that I shouldn't take on any loans? My sweet, it's not possible to do without them; things are already bad with me, and, who knows, what if something were to go wrong with you! You're weak, after all; so that's what I'm writing about, the fact that I must definitely borrow. Well, so I continue.

I'll mention to you, Varvara Alexeyevna, that in the office I sit next to Yemelyan Ivanovich. That's not the same Yemelyan that you know. This one is a titular counsellor, just as I am, and he and I are pretty much the veteran soldiers, the oldest in the department. He's a kind soul, an unselfish soul, but he's not very talkative and always looks like a real bear. On the other hand he's businesslike, his pen produces a pure English script, and to tell the whole truth, his handwriting is not inferior to mine – a worthy man! We've never been close, but just exchanged the customary goodbyes and hellos; and if at times I've needed a penknife, then I've had occasion to ask him: 'Yemelyan Ivanovich, will you give me a penknife?', in short, it's been only what communal life demands. So today he says to me: 'Makar Alexeyevich,' he says, 'why so deep in thought?' I can see that the man wishes me well, so I opened up to him, 'it's like this, Yemelyan Ivanovich', that is I didn't tell him everything, and God forbid that I ever should, because I haven't the heart to tell it, but I opened up to him about some things, told him things were tight and the like. 'You should borrow, old chap,' says Yemelyan Ivanovich, 'you could even borrow from Pyotr Petrovich, he makes loans on payment of interest; I've borrowed from him; he charges a decent rate, not too onerous.' Well, Varenka, my little heart leapt. I keep thinking perhaps the Lord will speak to my bene-factor Pyotr Petrovich's heart, and he'll make me a loan. I'm already calculating myself how I'd go and pay my landlady, and help you, and smarten myself up all round, otherwise it's so shameful: it's dreadful just sitting in my place, apart from the fact that our scoffers laugh, God forgive them! And His Excellency sometimes passes by our desk; well

God forbid that he should glance at me and notice that I'm improperly dressed! The most important thing for him is being clean and tidy. Perhaps he wouldn't even say anything, but I'd die of shame – that's the way it would be. As a result of which, pulling myself together and hiding my shame in my ragged pocket, I made for Pyotr Petrovich, both filled with hope and petrified by expectation – all at the same time. Well then, Varenka, you know, it all ended in a nonsense! He was busy with something, speaking with Fedosey Ivanovich. I went up to him from the side and tugged at his sleeve, and said 'Pyotr Petrovich, I say, Pyotr Petrovich!' He glanced around, and I continue: 'well, it's like this, thirty roubles or so' etc. It was as if he didn't understand me at first, and then when I explained everything to him he laughed, and then nothing, he fell silent. I said the same thing to him again. And he says to me – 'Do you have security?' And then he buried his nose in his document, writing and not looking at me. I was rather lost for words. No, I say, Pyotr Petrovich, I don't have any security, and I explain to him that 'as soon as I get my salary, I'll repay you, repay you without fail, I'll consider it my number one debt'. At this point somebody called for him, I waited for him, he came back and he started sharpening his quill, and doesn't seem to notice me. But I keep on about what I want – 'what, Pyotr Petrovich, isn't it possible somehow?' He's silent and it's as if he can't hear, I carry on standing there and I think, well, I'll give it a last try, and I tugged at his sleeve. If only he'd said something, but he finished sharpening his quill and then started to write; and I went away. You see, my dear, they may all even be worthy people, but they're proud, very proud – what am I to them? How can we compare with them, Varenka! That's why I've written you all this. Yemelyan Ivanovich laughed as well and shook his head, but then the good-hearted fellow did give me hope. Yemelyan Ivanovich is a worthy man. He promised to recommend me to a certain man; this man, Varenka, lives on the Vyborg Side, he makes loans on payment of interest too, he's someone in the fourteenth class. Yemelyan Ivanovich says that this one will be quite sure to make me a loan; I'll go tomorrow, my little angel, yes? What do you think? After all, there'll be trouble if I don't borrow! My landlady is all but driving me out of the apartment and won't agree to let me have dinner. Yes and my boots are in a dreadfully bad way, my dear, and I haven't got any buttons... well and that's not all I haven't got! Well and what if one of my superiors notices something so unseemly? Calamity, Varenka, calamity, simply calamity!

Makar Devushkin

4TH AUGUST

Dear Makar Alexeyevich!

For God's sake, Makar Alexeyevich, borrow any amount of money just as quickly as you can; I wouldn't have asked you for help in my present circumstances for anything, but if you knew what my position is! There's no way we can remain in this apartment. The most dreadfully unpleasant things have happened to me, and if you only knew what a state of upset and agitation I'm in now! Imagine, my friend: this morning we are visited by an unknown man of advanced years, almost an old man, wearing his medals. I was surprised, and didn't understand what he wanted of us. Fedora had gone out to the shop at the time. He began questioning me about how I lived and what I did and, without waiting for a reply, he announced to me that he was the uncle of that officer; that he was very angry with his nephew for his bad behaviour and for getting us a bad name throughout the building; he said his nephew was just a little boy and a windbag, and that he was prepared to take me under his wing; he advised me not to listen to young men, added that he commiserated with me like a father, that he had paternal feelings for me and was prepared to help me in everything. I'd turned completely red, didn't even know what to think, but didn't hurry to thank him. He forcibly took hold of my hand, gave my cheek a tweak, said that I was very pretty and that he was extremely pleased with the fact that I had dimples on my cheeks (God knows what he was saying!), and finally he tried to kiss me, saying that he was only an old man (he was so disgusting!). At this point Fedora came in. He became rather embarrassed and started saying once more that he felt respect for me because of my modesty and moral behaviour and that he very much wished that I wouldn't shun him. Then he called Fedora aside and under some strange pretext tried to give her a sum of money. Naturally,

Fedora didn't take it. Finally he prepared to go home, repeated all his assurances once again, said that he would come and see me once again and bring me earrings (he himself seemed very embarrassed); he advised me to change my apartment and recommended a splendid apartment to me, one he had his eye on and which would cost me nothing; he said he had taken a great liking to me, since I was an honest and sensible girl, he advised me to beware of profligate youths, and finally announced that he knew Anna Fyodorovna, and that Anna Fyodorovna had instructed him to tell me that she would be visiting me herself. At this point everything became clear. I don't know what happened to me; for the first time in my life I was experiencing such a situation; I was beside myself; I completely covered him in shame. Fedora helped me and almost drove him from the apartment. We decided that this was all the doing of Anna Fyodorovna: otherwise how could he have known about us?

Now I'm turning to you, Makar Alexeyevich, and begging you for help. For God's sake don't abandon me in such a situation! Please borrow, get hold of at least some sum of money, we have no means to leave the apartment and it's quite impossible to remain here any longer: Fedora's advice is the same. We need at least some twenty-five roubles; I'll repay the money to you; I'll earn it; Fedora will get me some more work in a few days' time, so that if you're charged a high rate of interest, pay no attention to that and agree to everything. I'll repay it all to you, only for God's sake don't deny me your help. It costs me a lot to trouble you now when you're in such circumstances, but all my hopes are pinned on you alone! Goodbye, Makar Alexeyevich, think of me, and God grant you success!

V. D.

4TH AUGUST

Varvara Alexeyevna, sweetheart!
It's all these unexpected blows that shake me! It's such awful misfortunes that are killing my spirit! Apart from the fact that this mob of various lickspittles and good-for-nothing old men want to put you in

your sickbed, my little angel, apart from all that – they, these lickspittles, they want to destroy me as well. And they will destroy me, I give my word on it, they'll destroy me! I mean, even now I'm prepared to die sooner than not help you! If I don't help you, then that's already death for me, Varenka, that's already death, pure and simple, but if I do help, then you'll fly away from me, like a little bird from its nest that these owls, these predatory birds are ready to peck to death. That's what's tormenting me, my dear. Yes and you, Varenka, how cruel you are! How could you do it? You're being tormented, hurt, you're suffering, my little fledgling, and still you grieve that you have to trouble me, and, what's more, promise to work off your debt, that is, to tell the truth, you're going to wear yourself out with your poor health so as to come to my aid in time. I mean, Varenka, just you think of what you're saying! Why should you be sewing, why should you be working, tormenting your poor little head with worries, damaging your pretty little eyes and ruining your health? Ah Varenka, Varenka, don't you see, sweetheart, I'm good for nothing, and I know myself that I'm good for nothing, but I'll make myself good for something! I'll overcome everything, I'll find some work on the side myself, I'll copy out various papers for various men of letters, I'll go and see them, I'll go myself, I'll force them to give me work; because you know, my dear, they look for good scribes, I know they look for them, but I won't let you wear yourself away; I won't let you carry out such a pernicious intention. I shall take a loan without fail, my little angel, and I shall sooner die than not take a loan. And you write, my sweetheart, that I shouldn't take fright at a high rate of interest – and I won't take fright, my dear, I won't take fright, I won't take fright at anything now. I'll ask for forty paper roubles, my dear; after all, that's not a lot, Varenka, what do you think? Can I be trusted with forty roubles from the word go? That is, I mean, do you think me capable of inspiring confidence and trust at first sight? From my face, from the first glance, is it possible to make a favourable judgement about me? You try and remember, little angel, am I capable of inspiring? What do you on your part suppose? Do you know, I feel such fear – it's morbid, if truth be told, it's morbid! From the forty roubles I'll set twenty-five aside for you, Varenka; two silver roubles for the landlady, and the rest is intended for my personal expenditure. You see, the landlady ought to be given a bit more besides, it's even essential; but you take the whole matter into consideration, my dear, run through all my needs, then you'll see there's simply no possible way of giving more, consequently there's no point even talking about it, and there's no need even to mention it. I'll buy boots for a silver rouble; I don't even know now whether I'll be able to appear at work tomorrow in the old ones. A neckerchief would also be essential, for the old one will soon be a year old; but since you promised to cut me not only a kerchief, but also a shirt-front from your old apron, I shan't even think any more about clothes. So then, I've got boots and a kerchief. Now buttons, my friend! After all, you must agree, my little mite, that I can't be without buttons; but almost half have come off down one side of my coat! I tremble at the thought that His Excellency might notice such disorder and say – well what will he say? I won't even hear, my dear, what he'll say, for I'll die, die, die on the spot, really, I'll go and die of shame at the idea alone! Oh, my dear! So then after all the essentials there'll still be three roubles left; so then that will be for expenses and for half a pound of tobacco; because, my little angel, I can't live without tobacco, and it's already nine days now that I've not had my pipe in my mouth. To be honest, I'd have bought it and said nothing to you, but I'd have felt ashamed. There you are with problems, you're deprived of the very last essentials, and I'm here enjoying various pleasures; so that's why I'm telling you all this, so that the pangs of conscience shouldn't torment me. I openly admit to you, Varenka, I'm now in an extremely needy state, that is absolutely nothing of the kind has ever happened to me before. My landlady despises me, there's no respect at all from anyone; the most awful deficiencies, debts; and at work, where even before I didn't have an easy time from my fellow-clerks – now, my dear, it goes without saying. I hide it, I painstakingly hide everything from everyone, and I hide myself, and when I go in to work, then it's sidling, I keep away from everyone. You know, it's only to you that I have the strength of spirit to confess it… Well then, how could he not give me it! Well no, Varenka, better not even think about it and not kill my spirit with such thoughts in advance. That's why I'm writing this, to forewarn you that you shouldn't think about this yourself and torment yourself with a wicked idea. Ah my God, what will happen to you then? It's true that then you won't leave this apartment, and I'll be with you – but no, I won't even return then, I'll simply vanish somewhere, disappear. Here I am writing away to you, whereas I need to have a shave, well, it looks a lot better, and a good appearance always gets its way. Well, God grant! I'll say a prayer and be off!

M. Devushkin

5TH AUGUST

Dearest Makar Alexeyevich!
You at least shouldn't despair! There's enough sorrow as it is. I'm sending you thirty kopeks in silver; I can't possibly manage any more. Buy yourself what you need most to stay alive somehow until tomorrow at least. We ourselves have almost nothing left, and I just don't know what will happen tomorrow. It's sad, Makar Alexeyevich! But anyway, don't be sad; it didn't work, so what can you do? Fedora says it's not such a bad thing, for the time being we can even stay in this apartment, and even if we'd moved, we'd only have saved a little, and if they want to, then they'll find us anywhere. Only it's still unpleasant somehow staying here now. If I weren't sad, I'd write you something.

What a strange character you have, Makar Alexeyevich! You take everything too much to heart; as a result you'll always be the most unhappy man. I read all your letters carefully and can see that in every letter you torment and worry yourself about me as you have never been worried about yourself. Everyone will say, of course, that you have a kind heart, but I'll say that it's simply too kind. I'm giving you some friendly advice, Makar Alexeyevich. I'm grateful to you, very grateful for all that you've done for me, I feel it all very much; so judge, then, how it feels for me to see that even now, after all your misfortunes, of which I was the unwitting cause, even now you only live courtesy of what I'm living through: through my joys, my sorrows, my heart! If you take everything to do with another person so to heart, and if you're so sympathetic about everything, then truly, there is every reason to be the most unhappy man. Today, when you came in to see me after work, I had a fright looking at you. You were so pale, terrified, desperate: you looked awful – and all because you were afraid of telling me about your failure, afraid of distressing me, frightening me, and when you saw that I all but burst out laughing, almost the whole weight was lifted from your heart. Makar Alexeyevich, don't be sad, don't despair, be more reasonable – I beg you, I implore you. Well, you'll see that everything will be fine, everything will change for the better; otherwise your life will be hard, forever in anguish and pain over someone else's sorrow. Goodbye, my friend; I implore you, don't worry too much about me.

V. D.

5TH AUGUST

Sweetheart, Varenka!
Well alright, my little angel, alright! You've decided it's not such a bad thing that I didn't get any money. Well alright, I'm calm, I'm happy on your account. I'm even glad you're not abandoning me, an old man, and will stay in this apartment. And if I'm telling the whole truth, then my heart was all overflowing with joy when I saw that you'd written so nicely about me in your little letter and given due praise to my feelings. I say this not out of pride, but because I can see how you love me if you worry so about my heart. Well alright; what can you say now about my heart? The heart looks after itself; but you instruct me, my dear, not to be faint-hearted. Yes, my little angel, perhaps I'll say myself that it's unnecessary, this faint-heartedness; but for all that, my dear, decide for yourself what boots I'll go to work in tomorrow! That's the thing, my dear; and after all, a thought like that can destroy a man, completely destroy him. But the main thing is, my dear, it's not for myself I grieve, not for myself I suffer; it's all the same to me, even going around in a hard frost without a greatcoat and without boots, I'll suffer and endure it all, it's alright for me; I'm a simple little man – but what will people say? My enemies, all those wicked tongues, what will they start saying when you set off without a greatcoat? I mean, it's for people that you go around in a greatcoat, and I suppose you wear boots for them too. In that case, my

dear, my little sweetheart, I need boots to uphold my honour and my good name; whereas in boots full of holes both the one and the other are lost – believe me, my dear, believe my many years of experience; listen to me, an old man who knows the world and people, and not to any old daubers and scribblers.

But I still haven't even told you in detail, my dear, how it really all was today, what I had to go through today. What I went through, the amount of spiritual pressure I endured in one morning, was what another man wouldn't endure even in an entire year. This is the way it was: I set out, firstly, ever so early, so as both to catch him and be in time for work. There was such rain, there was such slush today! I huddled inside my greatcoat, my little flower, and I'm walking and walking and thinking all the time: 'Lord, forgive me my trespasses and send the fulfilment of my desires.' I went past the *** church, crossed myself, repented of all my sins, and remembered that I wasn't worthy to come to arrangements with the Lord God. I sank into myself and didn't want to look at anything; and so I went on without looking where I was going. The streets were empty, and everyone I did meet was so busy, so careworn, and no wonder: who'd go walking at such an early hour and in such weather! I ran into an artel of dirty workmen; they jostled me, these ruffians! I came over timid, it was getting dreadful, to tell the truth I didn't even want to think about money – let it just be on the off-chance! Right by the Voskresensky Bridge my sole came off, so I just don't know myself what I walked on then. And at this point I ran into our assistant clerk Yermolayev, he pulled himself erect and stands there, following me with his eyes as if asking for a tip; ah my dear fellow, I thought, a tip, how could I give you a tip! I got awfully tired, stopped for a moment and had a bit of a rest, and then dragged myself on again. I gazed around on purpose to find something to stick my thoughts to, to distract me, to cheer me up: not a chance – I couldn't attach a single thought to anything, and in addition I'd got so filthy that I began to feel ashamed of myself. Finally in the distance I caught sight of a wooden house, yellow and with an attic storey like a belvedere – right, well, I think, that's it, that's like Yemelyan Ivanovich said – Markov's house. (It's this Markov, my dear, that lends money at a rate of interest.) I was quite beside myself now, and I mean I knew it was Markov's house, but still I asked the duty policeman, 'Whose is that house, old boy?' The policeman's so rude, speaks unwillingly as if he's angry with someone, mutters his words through clenched teeth – that, he says, that's Markov's house. These policemen are all so insensitive – but what's the policeman to me? But it was all somehow bad and unpleasant impressions, in short, it was all one thing leading to another; from everything you can draw something similar to your own situation, and it's always like that. I walked up and down the street past the house three times, and the more I walk, the worse it gets – no, I think, he won't give me it, he won't give me it for anything! First, I'm a stranger, then mine is a delicate matter, and then I don't cut a very good figure – well, I think, as fate decides; just so as not to regret it later on, after all, I won't get my head bitten off for trying – and I quietly opened the gate. And at this point another misfortune: a stupid, nasty little yard dog attached itself to me; it's barking itself out of its skin! And it's rotten, trivial things like that that always infuriate a person, my dear, and make him come over timid, and destroy all the decisiveness that he'd thought about in advance; so I went into the house petrified, went in and straight into another misfortune – I failed to make out what was on the ground in the murk by the doorstep, took a pace and stumbled over some woman, and the woman was decanting milk from a milk-pail into jugs and she spilt all the milk. And the stupid woman began shrieking and jabbering – 'and where do you think you're going, sir, what do you want?' and then she set off moaning, something about the devil. And what's more I notice, my dear, that in matters of a similar kind something of the sort has always happened to me; you know, it must just be my fate; I'm forever getting sidetracked by something. The mistress, an old witch of a Finn, poked her head out at the noise and I turned directly to her – 'Does Markov live here?' No, she says; she stood a minute, giving me a good look. 'And what do you want with him?' I explain to her that it's like this, Yemelyan Ivanovich – well and all the rest of it – I've got a little business, I say. The old woman called her daughter, and her daughter came out too, no youngster, bare-footed – 'call your father; he's upstairs with the lodgers – come in, please.' I went in. Not a bad room, pictures hanging on the walls, all portraits of some generals or other, there's a sofa, a round table, mignonette, balsam – and I keep on thinking, 'that's enough, shouldn't I clear off while the going's good, should I go or not?' And you know, my dear, I really did want to run away! Better, I'm thinking, if I come tomorrow; the weather will be better, and I can wait – whereas today there's the milk that's been spilt, and the generals are looking so cross… I was already heading for the door, but in he came – nothing special, grey-haired, furtive little eyes, in a dirty dressing-gown tied with a rope. He enquired why and how, and I said, 'It's like this: Yemelyan Ivanovich – forty roubles or so', I say; 'that sort of thing' – but I didn't finish. I could see by his eyes that it was a lost cause. 'No,' he says, 'what business is this, I've got no money; what then, have you some security or something?' I began to try explaining 'I've no security, but Yemelyan Ivanovich' – in short, I explain what's necessary. After listening to it all, 'no,' he says, 'what about Yemelyan Ivanovich! I've got no money.' Well, I think, so be it then; I knew all this, I foresaw it – well, Varenka, it would simply have been better if the ground had opened up beneath me; this cold feeling, my legs numb, goose-flesh up and down my back. I'm looking at him, and he's looking at me and all but saying 'well, be on your way, my man, there's nothing for you here' – so that if something of the kind happened another time, I'd be utterly shamefaced. Well what do you want, what do you need the money for? (That's what he was asking, you see, my dear!) I tried to open my mouth, just so as not to stand there to no purpose, but he didn't begin to listen to me – no, he says, I've got no money; it would be my pleasure, he says. I kept on presenting it to him, I'm saying I only want a little, after all, I'll pay it back, I say, I'll pay it back on time, I'll pay it back even before it's due, he could ask any interest he liked and I swear to God I'll pay it back. At this moment I remembered you, my dear, I remembered all your misfortunes and needs, I remembered your fifty kopeks – no, he says, who cares about interest, but if there were security, now! Because I've got no money, I swear to God I haven't; it would be my pleasure, he says – he even swore, the scoundrel!

Well, at this point, my dear, I don't even recall how I left, how I crossed the Vyborg Side, how I got to Voskresensky Bridge, I was dreadfully tired, I was frozen stiff, chilled to the marrow, and I only managed to arrive at work at ten o'clock. I wanted to clean myself up a bit, get rid of the dirt, but Snegirev, the watchman, said I couldn't, 'you'll

ruin the brush,' he says, 'and the brush, sir, belongs to the department.'
That's the way they are now, my dear, so for these gentlemen too I'm
little better than a bit of rag you wipe your feet on. I mean, what is it that
kills me, Varenka? It's not the money that kills me, but all these little
alarms of life, all these whispers, little smiles, little jokes. His Excellency
might unexpectedly have something to say on my account sometime –
oh, my dear, my golden age is over! I've reread all your letters today; I
feel sad, my dear! Goodbye, my dear, may the Lord preserve you!

M. Devushkin

PS I wanted to describe my sorrow to you, Varenka, with a bit of funny
stuff mixed in, only I evidently can't manage it, the funny stuff. I wanted
to please you. I'll come and see you, my dear, I'll be sure to come, I'll
come tomorrow.

11TH AUGUST

Varvara Alexeyevna! My sweetheart, my dear! I'm ruined, we're both
ruined, we're both of us irrevocably ruined together. My reputation,
pride – all is lost! I am destroyed and you are destroyed, my dear, and you
and I together are irrevocably destroyed! It is I, I that have led you to
destruction! I am persecuted, my dear, despised, held up to mockery, and
my landlady has simply begun abusing me; she shouted and shouted at
me today, gave me such a roasting, set me lower than a splinter. And at
Ratazyayev's in the evening one of them began reading out loud the draft
of a letter that I wrote to you but accidentally let drop out of my pocket.
Oh madam, how they jeered! They called out our names, called them out
and they roared and roared with laughter, the traitors! I went in to them
and condemned Ratazyayev for his treachery; I told him he was a traitor!
And Ratazyayev replied that I was a traitor myself, that I was busy with
various conquests; 'you were hiding yourself from us,' he says, 'you're a
Lovelace'; and now they all call me Lovelace, and I don't have any other
name! Do you hear, my little angel, do you hear – now they know
everything, they're familiar with everything, and they know about you,
my dear, and everything there is to know about you, they know about

everything! And that's nothing! Faldoni's the same, he's in it with them as well; I sent him to the sausage shop to get something today; he simply won't go, he says he's got something to do! 'But it's your duty to go,' I say. 'No, it's not,' he says, 'it's not my duty, you don't pay my mistress any money, so I don't have any duty towards you.' I wasn't going to take an insult from him, from an uneducated peasant, and I called him a fool; and he says to me – 'it takes one to know one.' I thought he must have been drinking to say something so rude to me – and so I say to him, 'You're drunk, you peasant, you!' And he says to me, 'Was it you that treated me or something? Have you got the money for the hair of the dog yourself? You yourself have to beg ten kopeks at a time off some woman,' – and then added: 'Huh! And still think you can give orders!' There, my dear, that's what things have come to! I'm ashamed to be alive, Varenka! I'm like a man possessed; worse than some tramp without a passport. Grave calamities! I'm lost, simply lost! Irrevocably lost.

M. D.

13TH AUGUST

Dearest Makar Alexeyevich! It's just trouble after trouble coming down on us, I just don't even know myself what to do! What will happen to you now? And I can't be relied on; I burned my left hand today with the iron; I accidentally dropped it, and hurt and burned my hand all at the same time. There's no way I can work, and Fedora has been sick for three days now. I'm in agonies with worry. I'm sending you thirty kopeks in silver; that's almost all we have left, but God knows how I should like to help you now with your needs. It's upsetting to the point of tears! Goodbye, my friend! It would be a great consolation to me if you were to visit us today.

V. D.

Makar Alexeyevich! What is the matter with you? You must have lost the fear of God! You're simply driving me mad. Aren't you ashamed of yourself? You're ruining yourself, just think of your reputation! You're an honourable, noble, proud man – well, when everyone finds out about you! You'll simply have to die of shame! Or do you feel no pity for your grey hairs? Well, do you fear God? Fedora said she'd no longer help you now, and I won't be giving you any money either. What have you brought me to, Makar Alexeyevich! You probably think it's nothing to me that you're behaving so badly; you don't know yet what I endure because of you! I can't even go up and down our staircase: everybody looks at me, they point their fingers at me and say such terrible things; yes, they say bluntly that *I'm mixed up with a drunkard.* How do I feel hearing that! When they bring you back, all the tenants point you out with contempt: there, they say, they've brought back that civil servant. And I just can't say how ashamed I feel for you. I swear to you that I shall move away from here. I'll go and work as a maid somewhere, as a laundrywoman, but I won't stay here. I wrote and asked you to call on me, but you didn't call. Evidently my tears and requests are nothing to you, Makar Alexeyevich! And where did you get the money from? For God's sake, look after yourself. You'll be ruined, you'll be ruined for nothing! And what shame and dishonour! Your landlady didn't even want to let you in yesterday, you spent the night just inside the porch: I know everything. If you knew how hard it was for me when I found all this out. Come and visit us, you'll have a nice time here: we'll read together, we'll reminisce about the old days. Fedora will tell us about her wanderings as a pilgrim. For my sake, my dear, don't ruin yourself and don't ruin me. It's just for you alone, you know, that I live, for your sake that I stay with you. And now you're like this! Be an honourable man, firm in misfortune; remember that poverty is no sin. Yes and why despair? This is all temporary! God willing, everything will come right, only you stand firm now. I'm sending you twenty kopeks, buy yourself some tobacco or whatever you like, only for God's sake don't spend it on anything bad. Come and visit us, be sure to come. Perhaps you'll be ashamed like before, but don't you be ashamed, it's false shame. If only you'd bring true repentance. Trust in God. He will arrange everything for the best.

V. D.

Varvara Alexeyevna, my dear!

I'm ashamed, my little flower, Varvara Alexeyevna, I'm utterly shame-faced. But then what's so out of the ordinary in this, my dear? Why shouldn't you bring a little cheer to your heart? I don't even think about my soles then, because a sole is nonsense and will always remain a simple, dirty, rotten sole. And boots are nonsense too! And the Greek sages went about without boots, so why should the likes of us make a fuss over such an unworthy object? So in that case why should people offend me, why should they despise me? Ah, my dear, my dear, you found what to write! And tell Fedora that she's a cantankerous, troublesome, hot-headed woman, and in addition she's stupid, in-expressibly stupid! And as far as my greyness is concerned, you're wrong about that too, my dear, because I'm not at all such an old man as you think. Yemelya sends his regards. You write that you grieved and cried; and I write to you that I grieved and cried as well. In conclusion I wish you all good health and prosperity, and as far as I'm concerned, I'm also in good health and prosperous, and remain, my little angel, your friend

Makar Devushkin

Madam and dear friend, Varvara Alexeyevna!

I feel that I'm at fault, I feel that I've wronged you, and in my opinion there's nothing to be gained at all, my dear, from the fact that I feel all this, no matter what you say. Even before my misdemeanour I felt all this, but now my spirits have fallen, with the consciousness of guilt they've fallen. My dear, I'm not wicked and I'm not hard-hearted; but to torment your little heart, my sweet, I'd need to be neither more nor less than a bloodthirsty tiger, well and I've got the heart of a lamb and, as you know too, I don't have any urge towards bloodthirstiness; consequently, my little angel, neither am I totally to blame for my misdemeanour, just as neither my heart, nor my thoughts are to blame either; and so I don't even know what is to blame. It's such a murky business, my dear! You sent me thirty kopeks in silver, and then you sent me twenty kopeks; and my heart began to ache, looking at your orphan's money. You yourself have burned your hand, you'll soon be starving, but you write that I should buy some tobacco. Well, how was I to act in such an instance? Was I without a twinge of conscience, like a brigand, to start robbing you, a little orphan? It was at this point that my spirits fell, my dear, that is at first, feeling, like it or not, that I was good for nothing and that I was myself perhaps only a little better than my sole, I thought it unseemly to take myself for something meaningful, rather on the contrary, I began to think myself something unseemly and to a certain extent indecent. Well and when I lost respect for myself, when I allowed myself to deny my good qualities and my worth, then at that point everything went to ruin, at that point came the fall! It's already fated to be this way, and I'm not to blame for it. At first I went out for a bit of fresh air. And at that point it all happened, one thing on top of another: nature was so tearful, and the weather cold, and the rain, well and Yemelya happened by at that point. Varenka, he'd already pawned everything he had, everything of his had gone where it had to, and when I met him, he'd not had a bite to eat for two days already, and so now he wanted to pawn such things as you can't possibly even pawn, because things like that just aren't security. Well then, Varenka, I gave way more out of compassion for mankind than following my own bent. So that's how this sin happened, my dear! How he and I cried together! We talked about you. He's the kindest, he's a very kind man, and an extremely sensitive man. I feel all this myself, my dear; the reason all this sort of thing happens to me is that I feel all this a lot. I know, sweetheart of mine, how indebted I am to you! When I came to know you, I began firstly to know myself better as well, and I began to love you; whereas before you, my little angel, I was lonely, and it was as if I was asleep, and not alive in the world. They, my antagonists, said that even my figure was unseemly, and they found me repulsive, well, I began to find myself repulsive; they said I was dim, and I really thought I was dim, but when you appeared to me, you lit up the whole of my dark life, so that both my heart and my soul were lit up, and I acquired spiritual peace and found out that I too am no worse than anyone else; it's just that I don't shine in any way, I've got no polish, no tone, but nevertheless I am a man, in my heart and my thoughts I am a man. Well but now, feeling that I'm persecuted by fate, that, humiliated by it, I've allowed myself to deny my own worth, and depressed by my calamities, I've let my spirits fall. And since you now know everything, my dear, I humbly beg you not to show any more curiosity on this subject, for my heart is breaking and it's bitter and painful.

I assure you, my dear, of my esteem and remain your faithful

Makar Devushkin

3RD SEPTEMBER

I didn't finish the last letter, Makar Alexeyevich, because it was hard for me to write. Sometimes I have these minutes when I'm glad to be alone, to be sad alone, to pine alone, without sharing it, and such minutes are beginning to come upon me more and more frequently. There is something in my memories so inexplicable for me, that carries me away so uncontrollably, so powerfully, that for several hours at a time I can be senseless to all my surroundings, and I forget everything, everything in the present. And there is no impression in my present life, be it pleasant, difficult or sad, that cannot remind me of something similar in my past, and more often than not of my childhood, my golden childhood! But things always become hard for me after such moments. I become weak somehow, my dreaminess exhausts me, and even without that my health is becoming worse and worse.

But today the fresh, bright, brilliant morning, the likes of which are rare here in autumn, enlivened me, and I met it joyfully. And so it's autumn for us already! How I loved the autumn in the countryside! I was still a child, but even then I already felt a lot. I loved the autumn evening more than the morning. I remember, a stone's throw from our house was a lake at the bottom of a hill. This lake – it's as if I can see it now – was so broad and bright and pure, like crystal! Sometimes, if the evening was still, the lake was calm; nothing would stir on the trees that grew along the bank, the water was motionless as if it were a mirror. It's fresh and cold! The dew falls on the grass, little lights appear in the huts on the shore, the herd is driven home – and now I slip quietly out of the house to look at my lake, and sometimes I'd forget everything as I looked. The fishermen have some bundle of brushwood burning right beside the water, and the light pours a long, long way across the water. The sky is so cold and blue, and around the edges it's all streaked with fiery red bands, and these bands become paler and paler; the moon comes out; the air is so resonant, that if a frightened little bird takes off, or the reeds start rustling in the light breeze, or a fish splashes in the water – everything would be audible. White steam rises across the blue water, delicate, transparent. The distance darkens; everything is drowning somehow in the mist, while nearby everything is so sharply defined, as if cut with a chisel – a boat, the shore, the islands; some barrel, discarded, forgotten right by the shore, bobs a little on the water, a willow branch with yellowed leaves gets tangled in the reeds – a belated seagull flies up, then plunges into the cold water, then again flies up and sinks into the mist. I would forget everything, looking and listening – I was wonderfully happy! And I was still a child, a baby!...

I was so fond of the autumn – late autumn, when the grain has already been harvested, the work already finished, when people have already started gathering in their huts in the evenings, when everybody is already waiting for winter. Then everything becomes gloomier, the sky frowns with clouds, the yellow leaves settle like pathways around the edges of the bare wood, while the wood turns blue or black – especially in the evening, when a damp mist descends and the trees can be glimpsed through the mist like giants, like ugly, frightening ghosts. Sometimes you might be out late walking, you'd fall behind the others, you'd be walking by yourself, hurrying – it was horrible! You tremble like a leaf; any minute, you think, someone frightening will peer out of the hollow in that tree trunk; meanwhile the wind rushes through the wood, drones, roars and howls so mournfully, rips a cloud of leaves from the sorry branches, spins them around in the air, and beyond them birds rush by in a long, far-flung noisy flock, with wild piercing cries, so that the sky turns black and is completely covered by them. You become frightened, and now – it's exactly as if you can hear someone – there's somebody's voice, it's as if somebody is whispering: 'Run, run, child, don't be late; it'll be frightening here any minute, run, child!' Horror passes through your heart and you run and run until you're out of breath. You run home panting; the house is noisy and cheerful; we children are all given work: shelling peas or poppy-seeds. Damp firewood crackles in the stove; mother watches cheerfully over our cheerful work. My old nanny Ulyana tells stories about the old days or frightening fairy tales about wizards and dead men. We children squeeze together, girl to girl, but we all have a smile on our lips. Then suddenly we fall silent all at once… Hark! A noise! As if somebody's knocking! It was never anything; it's old Frolovna's spinning-wheel droning; how much laughter there was! And later on we can't sleep in the night from fear; we have such frightening dreams. Sometimes you'd wake up not daring to stir and you'd be frozen under the blanket until dawn. In the morning you'd get up as fresh as a daisy. You look out of the window: the whole field is covered in frost; a delicate autumnal rime hangs on the denuded boughs; the lake has a paper-thin layer of ice; white steam is rising across the lake; cheerful birds cry out. The bright rays of the sun shine all around and break up the thin ice like glass. It's light, bright and cheerful! In the stove the fire crackles once more; everybody sits down close to the samovar, while our black dog, Polkan, frozen through after the night, looks in through the windows and wags his tail amicably. A little peasant will ride past the windows on a jaunty little horse on his way to the wood for kindling. Everyone is so contented, so cheerful!… Ah, what a golden childhood I had!…

Now I've started crying like a baby, carried away by my memories. I called everything to mind so vividly, so vividly, the past all stood before me so brightly, while the present is so dull, so dark!… How will it end, how will it all end? Do you know, I have a sort of conviction, a sort of certainty that I'm going to die this autumn. I'm very, very sick. I often think about the fact that I'll die, but still I'd rather not die like this – and lie in the earth here. Perhaps I'll take to my bed again like I did then too, in the spring, but I've still not managed to recover. Even now I feel really bad. Fedora's gone out somewhere for the whole day today, and I'm sitting here alone. And for some time now I've been afraid of being left by myself; it constantly seems as if there's someone else in the room with me, as if someone's talking to me; especially when I fall deep in thought about something, then suddenly come to from my reverie, so that I start to feel afraid. That's why I've written you such a long letter; when I'm writing it passes. Goodbye: I'm ending the letter because I've got neither paper nor time. Of the money I made from my clothes and hat I've got only one silver rouble left. You gave your landlady two silver roubles; that's very good; she'll keep quiet now for a while.

Do something about your clothes somehow. Goodbye; I'm so tired; I don't understand why I'm becoming so weak; the slightest activity tires me. If some work turns up, how am I to do the work? That's what's killing me.

V. D.

5TH SEPTEMBER

Varenka, my sweet!

Today, my little angel, I experienced a lot of impressions. Firstly, my head ached all day. So as to revive myself somehow, I went out to take a walk along the River Fontanka. The evening was so dark and damp. Before six o'clock it's already getting dark – that's the way it is now! It wasn't raining, but on the other hand there was a mist as heavy as a good drop of rain. Storm clouds were crossing the sky in long, broad streaks. There were crowds of people walking along the embankment, and as if deliberately, the people had such ugly, depressing faces, drunken men, snub-nosed Finnish women with bare heads and wearing boots, artisans, cab drivers, the likes of me going about some business or other; little boys, some apprentice locksmith in a striped smock, hollow-cheeked and sickly, with a face bathed in smoked oil and with a lock in his hand; an ex-soldier, seven feet tall – that's what the people were like. It was evidently the sort of hour when no other people could have been there. It's like a shipping canal, the Fontanka! There's such a lot of barges, you can't work out where it could all fit in. On the bridges sit women with damp gingerbread and rotten apples, and they're all such dirty, damp women. It's miserable taking a walk along the Fontanka! Wet granite beneath your feet, at your sides – tall, dark, sooty buildings; beneath your feet the mist, above your head the mist as well. It was such a sad, such a dark evening today.

When I turned into Gorokhovaya Street, it was already completely dark and they'd started lighting the gas lamps. It's quite a long time since I've been on Gorokhovaya – I've not had the chance. It's a noisy street! What rich stalls and shops; everything simply shines and burns, material, flowers under glass, various hats with ribbons. You might think it's all just laid out to look pretty – but no; after all, there are people who buy all this and give it to their wives. It's a rich street! There are an awful lot of German bakers living on Gorokhovaya; they must be extremely well-off people too. How many carriages go by every minute; how does the roadway bear it all? Such smart coaches, glass like a mirror, inside – velvet and silk, noblemen's footmen wearing epaulettes and carrying swords. I looked into all the carriages, ladies sitting in all of them, so dressed-up, perhaps even princesses and countesses. It was probably the sort of hour when everyone was hurrying to balls and gatherings. It's curious seeing a princess and in general a grand lady close to; it must be very nice; I've never seen one; except like now, when you look into a carriage. At this point I thought of you. Ah my sweet, my dear! When I think of you now, my whole heart aches! Why are you, Varenka, so unfortunate? My little angel, in what way then are you worse than all of them? You're good, beautiful, educated; why then does such an evil fate befall your lot? Why does everything happen in such a way that a good person is in desolation, while happiness comes of its own accord to somebody else? I know, my dear, I know that it's not a good thing to think like this, that it's free thinking; but in sincerity, to tell the whole truth, why has the crow of fate croaked out a prophecy of happiness for one while he's still in his mother's womb, while another comes out into the world from the orphanage? And you know, it often happens that Ivan the Fool is the one that gets happiness. 'Ivan the Fool, you rummage in your grandfather's sacks, drink, eat, have fun, whereas you, you so-and-so, you just lick your lips; that's all you're good for, that's the way you are, brother.' It's a sin, my dear, it's a sin to think like this, but sin comes into your heart here somehow, like it or not. You too should ride in a carriage like that, my dear, my little flower. Generals would try to catch your gracious glance – not the likes of me; you'd go around not in a worn gingham dress, but in silk and gold. You wouldn't be thin and sickly like now, but like a sugar figure, fresh, rosy and plump. And then I'd be made happy just by the fact that I could at least glimpse you in brightly lit windows from the street, I could at least see your shadow; just at the thought that you were happy and cheerful there, my pretty little bird, I'd cheer up too. But now what? As if it wasn't enough that wicked people have ruined you, some scum, a libertine is offending you. The fact that his tailcoat sits smartly on him, that he looks at you shamelessly through a gold lorgnette, well, he gets away with everything, you even have to listen indulgently to his indecent talk! That's enough, isn't it, my dears? And why is all this so? It's because you're an orphan, because you're defenceless, because you have no powerful friend to give you decent support. But after all, what sort of person is it, what sort of people are they for whom it's nothing to insult an orphan? They're some sort of scum and not people, simply scum; they're nothing, they just make up numbers, but they're not there really, and I'm sure of that. That's how they are, these people! But in my opinion, my dear, that organ-grinder I met today on Gorokhovaya is more likely to inspire esteem than they are. He may go wandering around the whole day, waiting for some small change that's been lying idle, no use to anyone, to spend on food, but on the other hand he's his own master, he feeds himself. He doesn't want to beg for alms; but then he toils for people's pleasure, like a clockwork machine – 'there, I'll bring pleasure any way I can.' A beggar, he's a beggar, it's true, just the same beggar; but on the other hand he's a noble beggar; he's tired, he's frozen stiff, but still he toils, maybe in his own way, but nevertheless he toils. And there are many honest people, my dear, who earn perhaps just a little according to the measure and usefulness of their toil, but who bow to nobody and ask bread of no one. And I too, in exactly the same way as this organ-grinder, that is not in the same way, not at all like him, yet in my own way, in a noble, in a gentlemanly respect, in exactly the same way as he does, I toil as my strength allows, as best I can, so to speak. I can give no more, and what can't be cured must be endured.

The reason why I started talking about this organ-grinder, my dear, is that I happened to feel my poverty doubly today. I stopped to look at the organ-grinder. Such ideas were coming into my head – so I stopped to take my mind off things. I'm standing there, and there are cab drivers, some young woman, and a little girl as well, who's all dirty. The organ-grinder set himself up in front of somebody's windows. I notice a little one, a boy, around ten or so; he would have been a nice little thing, but to look at he's ill, sickly, wearing not much more than just a little shirt, all but barefooted he's standing, mouth wide open, listening to the music – childhood! He was so intent on watching the German's dolls dancing, while his own hands and feet were frozen, he's shivering and chewing the end of his sleeve. I notice he's got some little bit of paper in his hands. Some gentleman passed and threw the organ-grinder a small coin; the coin landed right in the box with a partition where a Frenchman's shown dancing with some ladies. No sooner had the coin jingled than my boy started, looked timidly around, and evidently thought it was me that had given the money. He ran up to me, his little hands are trembling, his little voice is trembling, he reached out the bit of paper to me and says: 'a note!' I unfolded the note – well so what, it's nothing new, it's: 'my benefactors, the children's mother is dying, three children are starving, so you help us now, then when I die, in return for your not forgetting my fledglings now, I won't forget you, my benefactors, in the other world.' Well what have we here; the matter's clear, it's an everyday matter, but what am I to give them? Well and I didn't give him anything. But how sorry I felt! A poor little boy, blue from the cold, perhaps hungry too, and he's not lying, I swear it, he's not lying; I know this business. But the only thing wrong is, why do these rotten mothers not look after their children, but send them out half-naked into such cold with notes? Perhaps she's a stupid woman, a weak character; and perhaps there's nobody to make the effort for her, and so she sits with her legs crossed, perhaps, and really is sick. Well, she should still go to the right place for help; but then perhaps she's simply a rogue who sends a hungry, sickly child out on purpose to deceive people, and makes him ill. And what will the poor boy learn with these notes? His heart only hardens; he goes running around, begging. People pass, but they've no time for him. Their hearts are made of stone; their words are cruel. 'Get away! Clear off! Stop messing about!' That's what he hears from everyone, and the child's heart hardens, and there shivers in vain in the cold a poor little browbeaten boy like a fledgling who's fallen out of a broken nest. His hands and feet are cold; it takes his breath away. You look, and there he is already coughing; not long to wait now, and the sickness will crawl into his chest like a snake, and then, before you know it, death is already standing over him, somewhere in a stinking corner, without care, without attention – and there you have the whole of his life! That's the way life can be! Oh, Varenka, it's torture to hear 'for the love of God' and pass by, and not give anything, and say to him 'God will give to you.' Another 'for the love of God' is nothing in comparison. (Even the words 'for the love of God' can be different, my dear.) One is long, drawn-out, habitual, memorised, quite beggarly; it's not such a torture not to give to this one, this is a long-term beggar who's been doing it for ages, a beggar by trade, this one is used to it, you think, he'll survive and knows how to survive. Yet another 'for the love of God' is unaccustomed, crude, frightening – just like today, when I was about to take the boy's note, there was someone standing right there by the fence, and he wasn't asking everyone, he says to me: 'Give me a coin, sir, for the love of God!' – and in such an abrupt, crude voice that some dreadful feeling made me shudder, but I didn't give him a coin: I didn't have one. And rich people don't like it either when poor men complain aloud about their hard lot – 'they're a nuisance', they say, 'they're importunate' – and poverty is always importunate: do their hungry groans stop them sleeping, or something?

To tell the truth, my dear, I began describing all this to you in part to get it off my chest, but more to show you an example of the good style of my writing. Because you'll probably acknowledge yourself, my dear, that recently my style has been taking shape. But now such anguish has come upon me that I've myself begun to sympathise to the depths of my soul with my ideas, and although I know myself, my dear, that this sympathy will get you nowhere, nevertheless in a certain way you'll do yourself justice. And honestly, my dear, you often destroy yourself without any reason, you don't value yourself at all and you grade yourself lower than a splinter. And if I express myself with a comparison, then perhaps it occurs because of the fact that I'm myself browbeaten and hounded, just like that poor little boy who asked me for charity. Now I'm going to talk to you, as an example, allegorically, my dear; just listen to me; there are occasions, my dear, early in the morning, hurrying to work, when I can't take my eyes off the city, the way it wakes up, rises, smokes, boils, clatters – and then sometimes you feel so small in the face of such a sight, that it's as if your inquisitive nose had been given a sort of tweak by somebody, and so you trudge on your way as quiet as a mouse and give it up as a bad job! Now look closely at what's going on in these big, black, sooty, solid buildings, go into it carefully, and then judge for yourself whether it was fair to grade yourself senselessly and fall into unworthy confusion. Note, Varenka, that I'm talking allegorically, not in a literal sense. Well, shall we see what's inside these buildings? There in some smoky corner, in some damp kennel, which, out of necessity, is thought of as an apartment, some workman has woken up from sleep; and all night, to give an example, he's been dreaming in his sleep of the boots that he'd accidentally got a hole in the day before, as if it were precisely such rubbish that a man ought to dream of! But then after all he's a workman, he's a cobbler: he can be forgiven for keeping on thinking about his own one subject. He's got his children whining and a hungry wife; and it's not only cobblers that get up like that sometimes, my dear. And that would be alright, and it wouldn't be worth writing about it, but here's what circumstance emerges at this point, my dear: right here, in this same building, a floor higher or lower, in gilded chambers, those same boots, perhaps, were also dreamed of by the richest of persons, that is a different manner of boots, of a different design, but boots all the same, for in the sense implied by me here, my dear, we all, my dear, turn out to be cobblers a little bit. And this would all be alright, but only the bad thing is that there's nobody alongside this richest of persons, no man who could whisper in his ear something like: 'that's enough, thinking of things like that, thinking only of yourself, living only for yourself, you're not a cobbler, your children are healthy and your wife isn't asking for something to eat; look around, can't you see a more noble object for your concern than your boots?' That's what I wanted to say to you allego- rically, Varenka. Perhaps it's too free a thought, my dear, but sometimes I have this thought, sometimes it comes, and then, like it or not, it breaks out of my heart as a burning word. And that's why there was no reason to value myself at next to nothing because I was frightened just by noise and thunder! I'll conclude then, my dear, with the suggestion that you might perhaps think I'm talking slander to you, or it's just that I'm feeling depressed, or I've copied this out from some book? No, my dear, don't you believe it – it's not so: I abhor slander, I'm not depressed and I've not copied anything out from any book – so there!

I arrived home in a sad frame of mind, sat down by the table, heated up my kettle and prepared to drink a glass or two of tea. Suddenly I see Gorshkov, our poor lodger, coming in to visit me. Even in the morning I'd noticed that he kept on darting in and out among the tenants and that he wanted to approach me. And in passing I'll say, my dear, that their existence is far worse than mine. Much worse! A wife, children! So that if I were Gorshkov, I just don't know what I'd do in his place! Well, so my Gorshkov came in, he bows, there's a little tear, as always, hanging on his lashes like puss, he shuffles his feet but can't get a word out of himself. I sat him down on a chair, on a broken one, it's true, but there wasn't any other. I offered him some tea. He made excuses, made excuses for a long time, however he finally took a glass. He was going to drink it without sugar, again began making excuses when I started assuring him that he must take some sugar, he argued for a long time, refusing, finally put the smallest little piece in his glass and started assuring me that the tea was uncommonly sweet. Ah, to what degradation does poverty bring people! 'Well then, what's up, old fellow?' I said to him. 'Well it's like this,' he says, 'Makar Alexeyevich, my benefactor, show God's charity, lend assistance to an unfortunate family; the wife and children, there's nothing to eat; what do you think that's like,' he says, 'for me, a father!' I tried to say something, but he interrupted me: 'I'm afraid of everyone here, Makar Alexeyevich,' he says, 'that is it's not that I'm afraid of them, but just, you know, I'm ashamed; they're all proud and arrogant. I wouldn't even think of troubling you,' he says, 'my good fellow and benefactor: I know you've had some problems yourself, I know you can't give a lot either, but give me at least something on loan; and the reason why,' he says, 'I dared to ask you, was that I know your kind heart, I know you've been in need yourself, that even now you're experiencing calamities yourself – and it's for that reason your heart feels compassion.' And he concluded with 'forgive my impertinence and impropriety, Makar Alexeyevich'. I reply to him that I'd be only too glad, but that I've got nothing, absolutely nothing. 'Makar Alexeyevich, old fellow,' he says to me, 'I'm not asking for a lot, it's just like this (at this point he went quite red), the wife,' he says, 'the children – going hungry – just ten kopeks or so.' Well, at this point my own heart began to ache. I think to myself, I'm easily outdone! But all that I had left was twenty kopeks, and I was counting on them: I meant to spend them the following day on my most pressing needs. 'No, my dear, I can't; it's like this,' I say. 'Makar Alexeyevich, old fellow, whatever you will,' he says, 'even ten kopeks.' Well, I took my twenty kopeks out of the drawer and gave them to him, my dear, a good deed, after all! Ah, poverty! I had a little chat with him: how is it, old fellow, I ask, that you're in such need, and yet even while being so needy you rent a room costing five silver roubles? He explained to me that he took the room six months before and paid the money for three months in advance; then later on such circumstances arose that the poor thing could go neither one way nor the other. He expected his case to come to an end by now. And his case is an unpleasant one. You see, Varenka, he's answerable before the court. He's in dispute with some merchant who cheated on a government contract; the deception was uncovered, the merchant put on trial, and he got Gorshkov, who also happened to be involved somehow, mixed up in his villainous business. But in truth Gorshkov is guilty only of negligence, of indiscretion and of an unforgivable failure to keep the government's interests in view. The case has already been going on for several years: Gorshkov keeps coming up against various obstacles. 'I'm innocent of the dishonesty of which I'm accused,' Gorshkov says to me, 'totally innocent, innocent of cheating and robbery.' This case has rather sullied him; he was dismissed from his position, and although he wasn't found to be fundamentally guilty, still until his complete vindication he's unable to obtain from the merchant some splendid sum of money that's due to him and which he's seeking before the court. I believe him, but the court doesn't trust his word; and it's the sort of case that's all so hooked up and knotted that you won't untangle it in a hundred years. No sooner do they untangle it a little than the merchant finds another hook and then another hook. I have heartfelt sympathy for Gorshkov, my dear,

I commiserate with him. A man without a post; he's not taken on anywhere because he's unreliable; what was held in reserve has been spent on food; the case is complicated, but in the meantime they had to live; and in the meantime without warning, quite inopportunely, a baby was born – well and there you have expenses: the son fell ill – expenses, he died – expenses; his wife is sick; he has some chronic illness: in short, he's suffered, he's suffered quite enough. He says, incidentally, that he expects a favourable resolution of his case in a few days' time, and that there's not even any doubt about it now. I feel sorry, sorry, so very sorry for him, my dear! I was kind to him. He's a lost and muddled man; he's looking for protection, so I was kind to him. Well, goodbye then, my dear. Christ be with you, keep well. My sweetheart! When I think of you, it's as if I hold some healing balm to my sick soul, and although I suffer for you, I find even suffering for you is easy.

Your sincere friend

Makar Devushkin

My dear, Varvara Alexeyevna!
I am beside myself as I write to you. I'm all agitated over a dreadful occurrence. My head's spinning. I feel that everything around me is spinning. Ah, my dear, what will I tell you now! This we didn't foresee. No, I don't believe I didn't foresee it; I foresaw it all. My heart sensed it all in advance! I even dreamed of something similar the other night.

This is what happened! I'll tell you without any style, but just as the Lord puts it into my heart. I went to work today. I arrived and I'm sitting writing. And you ought to know, my dear, that I was writing yesterday too. Well, so then yesterday Timofey Ivanovich comes up to me and is so good as to give me instructions personally, to the effect that 'the document's needed urgently'. 'Copy it, Makar Alexeyevich,' he says, 'neatly, quickly and accurately; it's going for signature today.' You should note, little angel, that I wasn't myself yesterday, didn't feel like looking at anything; such sorrow and anguish came over me! There was coldness in my heart and darkness in my soul; you were in my mind all the time, my little flower; well, I set about making the copy; I copied it neatly and well, only I just don't know how to put it to you more precisely, whether it was the devil himself that got into me, or whether it was determined by some secret fate, or whether it just had to happen that way – only I omitted a whole line; God knows what sense came of it, simply no sense at all came of it. They were late with the document yesterday and presented it to His Excellency for signature only today. I appear today at the usual hour as if nothing has happened and take my place alongside Yemelyan Ivanovich. You should note, dear, that recently I've begun to feel ashamed and suffer from embarrassment twice as much as before. Of late I've not even been looking at anybody. Someone's chair just has to scrape, and I'm already petrified. And that's just how it was today, I was sitting quiet, hunched, curled up like a hedgehog, and so Yefim Akimovich (such a troublemaker as the world had never seen before him) said so that all could hear: 'Makar Alexeyevich, why are you sitting there like this?' And then he pulled such a face that everyone that was near him and me simply fell about laughing, and it goes without saying, at my expense. And off they went, off they went! I laid back my ears, and I screwed up my eyes, and I sit there not stirring. That's my custom; that way they leave me alone sooner. Suddenly I can hear there's noise, running around, bustle; I can hear – or are my ears deceiving themselves? They're calling for me, they're demanding me, they're calling for Devushkin. My heart began to tremble in my breast, and I just don't know myself why I took fright; I only know that I took fright like never before in my life. I was rooted to my chair – and it was as if nothing was wrong, as if it wasn't me. But then they started again, closer and closer. And then it was right in my ear: 'Devushkin! Devushkin! Where's Devushkin?' I raise my eyes: Yevstafy Ivanovich is in front of me saying: 'Makar Alexeyevich, to His Excellency, quickly! You've made a mess of the document!' And it was just this one thing he said, but that was enough, wasn't it, my dear, enough had been said? I went numb, turned to ice, lost all feeling, and I went – well, I set off simply more dead than alive. I'm led through one room, through another room, through a third room, into his office – and I stood before him! I can't give you a positive report about what I was then thinking. I see His Excellency standing there and all of them around him. I don't think I bowed; I forgot. I was so dumbstruck that my lips were shaking and my legs were shaking. And not without reason, my dear. Firstly, I was ashamed; I glanced to the right at the mirror, and there was just every reason to go crazy at what I saw there. And secondly, I always behaved as if I was nowhere to be found on earth. So that His Excellency was scarcely aware of my existence. Perhaps he'd heard just in passing that they had a Devushkin in the department, but he'd never come into any close contact with him.

He began angrily. 'How could you, sir! What's that look for? A vital document, needed in a hurry, and you ruin it. And how could you,' – at this point His Excellency turned to Yevstafy Ivanovich. I only hear the sounds of the words reaching me: 'Negligence! Carelessness! Trouble-making!' I tried to open my mouth to say something. I'd have liked to ask forgiveness, but I couldn't, to run away – but I didn't dare try, and at this point... at this point, my dear, such a thing happened, that even now I can scarcely hold my pen from shame. My button – the devil take it – the button I had hanging by a thread – suddenly came off, fell, bounced (I'd accidentally knocked it, evidently), tinkled, and rolled away, the damned thing, straight, absolutely straight up to His Excellency's feet, and all this in the midst of universal silence! And that was all my justification, all my apology, all my reply, all I'd been intending to say to His Excellency! The consequences were dreadful! His Excellency immediately turned his attention to my figure and my clothes. I remembered what I'd seen in the mirror: I rushed to catch the button! I was that foolish! I bend down and try to pick up the button – it rolls, spins, I can't catch it, in short, I excelled myself as regards agility. It's at this point I feel that my last ounce of strength is leaving me, that now everything, everything is lost! The whole reputation is lost, the whole man is ruined! And at this point, for no reason at all, in both ears there's Tereza and Faldoni and everything starts ringing. Finally I caught the button, stood up, pulled myself erect, and if I'd not been such an idiot, I'd have stood there quietly at attention! But no: I started holding the button up to the dangling threads, as if it would attach itself as a result; and I'm smiling too, I'm smiling too. His Excellency turned away at first, then he glanced at me again – I hear him say to Yevstafy Ivanovich: 'How can it be?... Look at the state he's in! How can he!...

What has he!...' Ah, my dear, why this – how can he? And what has he? I'd excelled myself! I hear Yevstafy Ivanovich say: 'He's not been detected, not detected in anything, of exemplary behaviour, sufficient income, on the salary scale...' – 'Well, somehow alleviate for him,' says His Excellency. 'Give him an advance...' – 'He's taken it, so they say, he's taken it, taken it in advance in respect of such and such a period. Probably such circumstances, but of exemplary behaviour and not detected, never detected.' I was burning, my angel, I was burning in the fires of hell! I was dying! 'Well,' says His Excellency loudly, 'it's to be copied afresh quickly; Devushkin, come here, copy it afresh once more without any mistakes; and listen...' At this point His Excellency turned back to the others, gave out various orders, and everyone dispersed. No sooner had they dispersed than His Excellency hurriedly takes out his wallet, and from it a hundred-rouble note. 'There,' he says, 'any way I can, consider it as you wish...' – and he pressed it into my hand. I gave a start, my angel, my entire soul was shaken; I don't know what came over me; I almost tried to seize him by the hand. And he went quite red, my sweet, and – and here I'm not diverging even a hair's-breadth from the truth, my dear: he took my unworthy hand, and he shook it, he actually took it and shook it, as if it belonged to his equal, as if it belonged to a general like him himself. 'Off you go,' he says, 'any way I can... Don't make any mistakes, now it's just between ourselves.'

Now, my dear, this is what I've decided: I request you and Fedora, and if I had children I'd order them too, to pray to God, and this is how: you may not pray for your natural father, but you should pray every day and forever on behalf of His Excellency! I'll say one thing more, my dear, and I say this solemnly – pay good heed to me, my dear – I swear, that however I might be suffering from spiritual grief in the hard days of our misfortune, looking at you, at your calamities, and at myself, at my degradation and my incapability, despite all this I swear to you, that it's not so much the hundred roubles that are dear to me, as the fact that His Excellency himself was good enough to shake my unworthy hand, the hand of a drunkard, a wisp if straw! By doing so he gave me back to myself. By this deed he resurrected my spirit, made my life forever sweeter, and I'm firmly convinced, that no matter how sinful I am before the Almighty, still that prayer for the happiness and prosperity of His Excellency will reach His throne!…

My dear! I'm now in dreadful spiritual confusion, in dreadful agitation! My heart is beating and wants to leap out of my breast. And I myself seem to have gone all weak somehow. I'm sending you forty-five paper roubles, I'm giving twenty to my landlady, and I'm leaving myself thirty-five: I'll get my clothing seen to for twenty, and I'll leave fifteen to live on. But it's only now that all these impressions from the morning have shaken my whole existence. I'll lie down for a while. I do, however, feel calm, very calm. Only my soul aches, and deep down there I can sense my soul trembling, quivering, stirring. I'll come and see you; but now I'm simply drunk from all these sensations… God sees everything, my dear, my priceless little sweetheart!

Your worthy friend

Makar Devushkin

10TH SEPTEMBER

My dear Makar Alexeyevich!

I'm more glad than I can say about your good fortune and can appreciate the virtues of your superior, my friend. And so now you will have some rest from sorrow! Only for God's sake don't spend the money to no good purpose again. Live quietly, as modestly as possible, and right from today begin always putting at least something aside, so that misfortunes don't suddenly come upon you again. For God's sake don't worry about us. Fedora and I will survive somehow. Why did you send us so much money, Makar Alexeyevich? We don't need it at all. We're content with what we have. True, we shall need money soon to move out of this apartment, but Fedora hopes to be repaid an old debt by someone from long ago. Anyway, I'm leaving myself twenty roubles for extreme needs. The remainder I'm sending back to you. Please look after the money, Makar Alexeyevich. Goodbye. Live a calm life now, keep well and cheerful. I would write more to you, but I feel terribly tired, I didn't get out of bed the whole day yesterday. You did well, promising to drop in. Come and see me please, Makar Alexeyevich.

V. D.

My sweet Varvara Alexeyevna!

I beg you, my dear, don't part from me now, now, when I'm completely happy and content with everything. Sweetheart! Don't you listen to Fedora, and I'll do anything you like; I'll behave well, out of respect for His Excellency alone I'll behave well and responsibly; we'll write one another happy letters again, we'll confide to one another our thoughts, our joys, our worries, if we have any worries; we'll live together in harmony and happiness. We'll take up literature… My little angel! Everything in my fate has altered, and everything has altered for the better. My landlady has become more compliant, Tereza more intelligent, even Faldoni himself has become kind of nimble. I've made up with Ratazyayev. I went to him myself in sheer joy. He really is a nice chap, my dear, and the fact that people spoke badly of him, that was all rubbish. I've now discovered it was all a vile slander. He wasn't thinking of describing us at all: he told me so himself. He read me a new work. And the fact that he called me Lovelace that time, none of that was abuse or some unseemly name: he explained to me. It's taken word for word from a foreign language and means *a nimble chap*, and if you put it rather more prettily, rather more literarily, then it means *young fellow – keep it safe* – there! And not anything nasty. It was an innocent joke, my little angel. I, an ignoramus, was stupid enough to take offence. But now I've apologised to him… And the weather's so splendid today, Varenka, it's so nice. True, there was a bit of drizzle in the morning, as if it was being sprinkled through a sieve. Never mind! To make up for it, the air's become a little fresher. I went to buy some boots and bought an amazing pair of boots. I walked down Nevsky. I read *The Bee*[7]. Oh yes! I even forget to tell you about the main thing.

You see the thing is:

I had a conversation this morning with Yemelyan Ivanovich and Aksenty Mikhailovich about His Excellency. Yes, Varenka, it's not just me that that he's treated so charitably. He's been a benefactor not only to me, and is known to all the world for his kindness of heart. In many quarters praises are offered up in his honour and tears of gratitude are shed. He brought up an orphan. He was good enough to get her settled:

he gave her in marriage to a well-known man, a certain civil servant who was officer for special commissions in the service of His Excellency himself. He found a job in some office for the son of a certain widow and has done a lot more good deeds of various kinds. I, my dear, considered it my duty to put my own word in straight away and told everyone about His Excellency's deed for all to hear; I told them everything and concealed nothing. I hid my shame in my pocket. What shame could there be, what pride could there be in the face of such a circumstance? Right out loud – glory to the deeds of His Excellency! I spoke captivatingly, I spoke with fervour and I didn't blush, on the contrary, I was proud that I had to tell such a thing. I told about everything (I maintained a prudent silence only about you, my dear), about my landlady, and about Faldoni, and about Ratazyayev, and about boots, and about Markov – I told it all. A couple of them exchanged smiles, well, to tell the truth, they all exchanged smiles. Only it's probably in my figure they found something funny or on account of my boots – exactly, on account of my boots. But they couldn't have done it with any ill intent. It's just youth, or because of the fact that they're rich people, but they couldn't possibly have mocked my speech with any ill, any evil intent. Anything about His Excellency, that is – they couldn't possibly have done that. Isn't that so, Varenka?

I'm still unable to come to my senses somehow even now, my dear. All these events have confused me so! Do you have some firewood? Don't catch cold, Varenka; it doesn't take a moment to catch cold. Oh, my dear, you and your sad thoughts are killing me. I pray to God, how I pray to Him for you, my dear! For example, do you have woollen stockings, or anything warm in the way of clothes? Now, sweetheart, if you need anything, then for God's sake don't you go upsetting an old man. Just you come straight to me. The bad times are over now. Don't you worry on my account. Everything ahead is so nice and bright!

Yet it was a sad time, Varenka! But then it doesn't matter, it's over! The years will pass, and we'll just sigh about this time. I remember my young days. What! There were times I didn't have a kopek. I was cold and hungry, but cheerful, and that's that. You'd walk down Nevsky in the morning, come across a pretty little face, and you were happy all day long. It was a great, great time, my dear! It's good to be alive in the world, Varenka! Especially in St Petersburg. Yesterday with tears in my eyes I repented before the Lord God and asked the Lord to forgive me all my sins in this sad time: my grumbling, liberal ideas, rowdy behaviour, hot-headedness. I remembered you fondly in my prayers. You alone, my little angel, fortified me, you alone consoled me, sent me on my way with good advice and instruction. I can never forget that, my dear. I kissed all your little notes today, my sweet! Well, goodbye, my dear. They say that somewhere not far from here there's clothing for sale. So I'll go and do a little enquiring. Goodbye, little angel. Goodbye.

Your sincerely devoted

Makar Devushkin

15TH SEPTEMBER

Dear Sir, Makar Alexeyevich!

I'm all in terrible agitation. Listen to what's happened here. I have a presentiment of something fateful. Judge for yourself, my priceless friend: Mr Bykov is in St Petersburg. Fedora met him. He was riding along, he ordered the droshky to be stopped, he approached Fedora himself and began enquiring where she lived. She didn't say at first. Then he said with a smirk that he knew who was living with her. (Anna Fyodorovna has evidently told him everything.) Then Fedora couldn't stop herself and right there in the street began reproaching him, chiding him, told him he was an immoral man, that he was the cause of all my misfortunes. He replied that it stands to reason that someone has misfortunes when they've got no money. Fedora told him I could have made a living by working, could have married, or else could have found a post of some sort, but that now my happiness was lost forever, and that what's more I was sick and would soon be dead. To this he remarked that I was still too young, that my head was still full of ideas, and *that our virtues too had grown tarnished* (his words).Fedora and I had thought that he didn't know where our apartment was, when suddenly yesterday, when I'd just gone out to Gostiny Dvor to do some shopping, he comes into our room; it seems he didn't want to catch me at home. He spent a long time questioning Fedora about our way of life;

114

examined all our things; looked at my work and finally asked: 'Who's this clerk that's acquainted with you?' At that moment you were going across the courtyard; Fedora pointed you out to him; he took a glance and gave a smirk; Fedora begged him to leave, told him that distress had already made me unwell as it was, and that it would be extremely unpleasant for me to see him in our home. He was silent for a while; he said he'd come because he had nothing else to do, and he tried to give Fedora twenty-five roubles; she, naturally, didn't take them. What could this mean? Why was it he visited us? I can't understand how he knows everything about us! I'm completely at a loss. Fedora says that her sister-in-law Aksinya, who comes to visit us, knows the laundress Nastasya, and Nastasya's cousin is a porter in the department where an acquaintance of Anna Fyodorovna's nephew works, so did some gossip perhaps creep over there? Actually, it's highly likely that Fedora's mistaken; we don't know what to think. Surely he won't come and visit us again! This idea alone horrifies me! When Fedora told me all this yesterday, I was so afraid that I almost fainted in fright. What else do they want? I don't want to know them now! What business do they have with poor me? Ah! How fearful I am now; I keep on thinking that Bykov will come in at any minute. What will happen to me? What else is fate preparing for me? For Christ's sake, come and see me right now, Makar Alexeyevich. Come and see me, for God's sake, come and see me.

V. D.

18TH SEPTEMBER

My dear, Varvara Alexeyevna!
There took place in our apartment this day an impossibly mournful, inexplicable and unexpected event. Our poor Gorshkov (you should note, my dear) has been completely vindicated. The judgement had already been made some time ago, but today he went to hear the final resolution. The case concluded extremely fortunately for him. Whatever blame lay upon him for negligence and carelessness – complete absolution was granted for everything. It was adjudged that a large sum of money should be obtained on his behalf from the merchant, so that

he's both much improved in his circumstances, and his honour has been cleared of any stain, and everything's become better – in short, he emerged with the most complete fulfilment of his desires. He came home today at three o'clock. He looked awful, he's white as a sheet, his lips are trembling, but he's smiling – he hugged his wife and children. A whole band of us went to his room to congratulate him. He was extremely touched by our action, bowed to all sides, shook each of us by the hand several times. It even seemed to me he'd grown too, and straightened up, and that there was no longer any little tear in his eyes. He was so agitated, the poor thing. He couldn't stay in the same place for two minutes; he picked up anything that came to hand, then dropped it again, smiled and bowed continually, sat down, stood up, sat down again, said God knows what – 'My honour,' he says, 'honour, good name, my children' – and the way he said it! He even started crying. We too for the most part shed a tear. Ratazyayev evidently wanted to encourage him and said: 'What's honour, my dear, when you have nothing to eat; money, my dear, money's the main thing; that's what you should thank God for!' – and at that point he patted him on the shoulder. It seemed to me that Gorshkov was offended, that is it wasn't that he expressed displeasure directly, but he just looked strangely somehow at Ratazyayev and removed his hand from his shoulder. And that wouldn't have happened before, my dear! Anyway, people have different characters. I, for example, wouldn't have shown myself to be arrogant at such a celebration; after all, my dear, sometimes even an unnecessary bow and you cause humiliation because of nothing more than an attack of kindness of spirit and an excess of softness of heart... but anyway, I'm not the one in question here! 'Yes,' he says, 'the money's a good thing too; thank God, thank God!' And after that, all the time we were with him, he kept repeating: 'Thank God, thank God!...' His wife ordered a fancier and more plentiful dinner. Our landlady herself cooked for them. Our landlady is in part a kind woman. But Gorshkov couldn't stay sitting in one place until dinner. He dropped into everyone's rooms, whether invited or not. He'd just go in, smile, sit down on a chair, say something, or sometimes not say anything – and leave. In the midshipman's room he even picked up the cards; and they sat him down to play the fourth hand. He played and played, made a nonsense of something in the game, played three or four times, then gave up playing. 'No,' he says, 'I wasn't serious, you know,' he says, 'I was just, you know.' – and left them. He met me in the corridor, took me by both hands, looked me straight in the eyes, only so oddly; he squeezed my hand and moved away, and still smiling, but smiling with difficulty somehow, strangely, like a dead man. His wife was crying with joy; everything was so cheerful in their room, festive. They'd soon had dinner. Then it's after dinner he says to his wife: 'Listen, darling, I'll just lie down for a while,' – and he went to his bed. He called his daughter to him, laid his hand on her head and spent a long, long time stroking the child's head. Then he turned to his wife again: 'And what about Petyenka? Our Petya,' he says, 'Petyenka?...' His wife crossed herself and replies that he's dead, you know. 'Yes, yes, I know, I know everything. Petyenka's in the kingdom of heaven now.' His wife can see that he's not himself, that he's been utterly shaken by what's happened, and says to him: 'You should go to sleep, darling.' – 'Yes, alright, in a moment I'll... just a little,' – at this point he turned away, lay for a while, then turned, tried to say something. His wife couldn't make out what he'd said and asked him: 'What, my friend?' But he doesn't reply. She waited a little – well, she thinks, he's fallen asleep, and she went out to spend an hour with the landlady. She returned an hour later – she sees her husband hasn't woken up yet and is lying there not stirring. She thought he was asleep, sat down and started doing some work. She tells how she worked for about half an hour and became so immersed in her reflections that she doesn't even remember what she was thinking about, she says only that she forgot about her husband. Only suddenly she came to with some sense of alarm and was struck first and foremost by the deathly silence in the room. She looked at the bed and sees that her husband is still lying in the same position. She went up to him, pulled the blanket off, looks – and he's already cold – he's dead, my dear, Gorshkov's dead, died suddenly, as if he'd been struck by lightning! But what he died of – God knows. I've been so overwhelmed by this, Varenka, that I still can't collect my thoughts. I can't believe it somehow that a man could die so simply. Such a poor, hapless man, this Gorshkov! Ah, fate, what a fate! His wife in tears, so frightened. The little girl's hidden herself in a corner somewhere. They've got such a commotion going on there, a medical investigation's to be carried out… I can't tell you for sure. Only it's a pity, oh, what a pity! It's sad to think that you really don't know the day or the hour… You perish like this for nothing…

Your

Makar Devushkin

Madam, Varvara Alexeyevna!

I hasten to inform you, my friend, that Ratazyayev has found me work with a certain author. Someone came to visit him and brought him such a thick manuscript – a lot of work, thank God. Only it's written so illegibly that I don't know how to set about the task; it's wanted quickly. It's all written about such things somehow that you can't even seem to understand it… We've agreed on forty kopeks a sheet. Why I'm writing you all this, my dear, is that now there'll be money on the side. Well, but goodbye now, my dear. I'm getting on with the work straight away.

Your faithful friend

Makar Devushkin

My dear friend, Makar Alexeyevich!

This is already the third day I've written nothing to you, my friend, but I've had many, many worries, and much anxiety.

Two days ago I had a visit from Bykov. I was alone, Fedora had gone out somewhere. I opened the door to him and was so frightened when I saw him that I was rooted to the spot. I sensed that I'd turned pale. He came in with a loud laugh as is his custom, took a chair and sat down. It was a long time before I could collect my thoughts, but finally I sat down in the corner at my work. He soon stopped laughing. My appearance seemed to shock him. I've grown so thin recently; my cheeks and eyes are sunken, I was as pale as my handkerchief… it really is hard for anyone who knew me a year ago to recognise me. He stared at me for a long time, but finally became cheerful once more. He said something or other, I don't remember what reply I gave him, and he started laughing again. He sat with me for a whole hour; he talked to me for a long time; asked some questions. Finally, before leaving, he took me by the hand and said (I'm writing it to you word for word): 'Varvara Alexeyevna! Between you and me, Anna Fyodorovna, your relative and my close acquaintance and friend, is a most vile woman.' (At this point he also called her by a certain indecent word.) 'She has both led your cousin astray, and ruined you. For my part, I too proved to be a villain in this instance, but then after all, it's an everyday business.' At this point he started chuckling for all he was worth. Then he remarked that he wasn't a master of eloquence, and that the main thing that needed to be explained, and about which he was enjoined not to remain silent by the obligations of honour, had now already been said, and that he was tackling the remainder in a few brief words. At this point he announced to me that he was seeking my hand, that he considered it his duty to restore my honour to me, that he was rich, that he would take me away after the wedding to his village in the steppe, that he wanted to go hare-hunting there; that he would never again return to St Petersburg, because St Petersburg was disgusting, that here in St Petersburg he had, as he himself expressed it, a good-for-nothing nephew, whom he had sworn to deprive of his inheritance, and specifically for this eventuality, that is wanting to have legitimate heirs, he was seeking my hand, that that was the main reason for his proposal. Then he remarked that I lived extremely poorly, that it was no wonder I was sick, living in such a hovel, foretold my inevitable death if I stayed like this even for another month, said that apartments in St Petersburg were disgusting, and finally asked if I needed anything.

I was so shocked by his proposal that, without knowing why myself, I burst into tears. He took my tears for gratitude, and told me he had always been sure that I was a kind, sensitive and educated girl, but that he had nonetheless resolved on this step only after finding out in the fullest detail about my present behaviour. At this point he asked a lot of questions about you, said that he had heard about everything, that you were a man of noble principles, that he on his part didn't want to be indebted to you, and would five hundred roubles be enough for you for all that you'd done for me? And when I explained to him that you'd done things for me that couldn't be paid for with any money, he told me that that was all nonsense, that that was all novels, that I was still young and read poetry, that novels are the ruination of young girls, that books only do damage to morality and that he couldn't bear any books; he advised me to live as long as he had and then to talk about people; 'then,' he added, 'you'll find out about people too.' Then he said that I should have a good think about his proposals, that it would be most unpleasant for him if I took such an important step unthinkingly, added that unthinking and emotional behaviour are the ruination of inexperienced youth, but that he very much wished for a favourable reply on my part, and that otherwise, finally, he would be forced to marry a merchant's widow in Moscow, because, he says, 'I've sworn to deprive my good-for-nothing nephew of his inheritance.' He insisted on leaving five hundred roubles on my tambour, to buy sweets, as he put it; he said I'd grow round as a doughnut in the country, that I'd live with him on the fat of the land, that he had an awful lot to do at the moment, that he'd been running around on business the whole day and that he'd popped in to see me now in a free moment. At this point he left. I've thought for a long time, I've given it a great deal of thought, I've been in torment, thinking, my friend, and finally I've made up my mind. My friend, I'm going to marry him, I have to consent to his proposal. If anyone can rid me of my shame, restore my honest name to me, stave off poverty, deprivation and misfortune from me in times to come, then it's he alone. What am I to expect from the future, what else can I ask of fate? Fedora says that you needn't lose your happiness; she says – what is it then in that case that's called happiness? I at least can't find another way for myself, my priceless friend. What am I to do? As it is I've completely ruined my health with work; I can't work all the time. Leave home to work? I'll waste away, pining, and what's more I won't satisfy anyone. I'm sickly by nature and so I'll always be a burden on other people's hands. Of course, I'm not bound for paradise even now, but what am I to do, my friend, what am I to do? What choice do I have?

I didn't ask you for advice. I wanted to think it through alone. The decision that you've just read is final, and I'm announcing it at once to

Bykov, who is hurrying me as it is for a final decision. He said his business won't wait, he needs to leave, and he can't delay things over trifles. God knows whether I'll be happy, my destiny is in His sacred, mysterious power, but my mind is made up. They say Bykov is a kind man; he'll respect me; perhaps I too shall also come to respect him. What more can be expected from our marriage?

I'm informing you of everything, Makar Alexeyevich. I'm sure you'll understand all my anguish. Don't try to deflect me from my intention. Your efforts will be in vain. Weigh up in your own heart everything that's forced me to act in this way. I was very troubled at first, but now I'm calmer. What lies ahead, I don't know. What will be, will be; as God wills!... Bykov has arrived; I'm leaving the letter unfinished. I wanted to say a lot more to you. Bykov's already here!

V. D.

23RD SEPTEMBER

My dear, Varvara Alexeyevna!

I hasten to reply to you, my dear; I hasten to announce to you, my dear, that I'm astonished. All this isn't right somehow... Yesterday we buried Gorshkov. Yes, it's so, Varenka, it's so; Bykov has acted honourably; only you see, my dear, the thing is, you're accepting. Of course, the will of God is in everything; it's so, it must be so without fail, that is the will of God must without fail be here; and the Providence of the Heavenly Creator is, of course, both good and mysterious, and destiny too, it's just the same. Fedora shows concern for you too. Of course, now you'll be happy, my dear, you'll enjoy prosperity, sweetheart, my little flower, my little beauty, my little angel – only you see, Varenka, how can it be so soon?... Yes, business... Mr Bykov has business – of course, who doesn't have business, and he might have some too... I saw him as he was leaving your apartment. A fine, fine figure of a man; even a very fine figure of a man. Only all this isn't right somehow, it's not really a matter of him being a fine figure of a man, and I'm somehow not myself either at the moment. Only how are we going to write letters to each other now? I, how am I to remain by myself? I'm weighing everything up, my little angel, I'm weighing everything up, as you wrote to me, I'm weighing it all up in my heart, these reasons. I was already finishing copying the twentieth sheet, and in the meantime these events turned up! My dear, I mean, you're going, so you'll need to do various bits of shopping, some shoes, a dress, and there's a shop I know too, incidentally, on Gorokhovaya; you remember how I kept describing it to you as well? But no! How can you, my dear, what do you mean? I mean, you can't leave now, it's just not possible, not possible at all. I mean, you need to do a lot of shopping, and get yourself a carriage. What's more, the weather's bad now too; you just look at the way the rain's pouring down, and it's such cold rain, and also… also the fact that you'll be cold, my little angel; your little heart will be cold! I mean, you're afraid of strangers, but you're leaving. And who will I be left with here by myself? And Fedora there says great happiness awaits you… but she's a troublesome woman, after all, and wants to ruin me. Will you be going to church tonight, my dear? I'd come along to look at you. It's true, my dear, absolutely true, that you're an educated, virtuous and sensitive girl, only let him rather marry the merchant's widow! What do you think, my dear? Let him rather marry the merchant's widow! As soon as it gets dark, my little Varenka, I'll just pop in to see you for an hour. It's getting dark early today, you know, and I'll just pop in. I'll be sure to come and see you for an hour today, my dear. You're expecting Bykov now, but as soon as he goes, then… Just wait, my dear, I'll pop in…

Makar Devushkin

27TH SEPTEMBER

My friend, Makar Alexeyevich!
Mr Bykov said that I should be sure to have enough holland for three dozen shirts. So seamstresses need to be found for two dozen as quickly as possible, and we have very little time. Mr Bykov is getting angry, he says there's an awful lot of fuss over these bits of clothes. Our wedding is in five days' time, and we're leaving the day after the wedding. Mr Bykov is in a hurry, he says there's no need to lose a lot of time over nonsense. The preparations have worn me out, and I can scarcely keep

on my feet. There's a dreadful amount to be done, but it really would be better if there were none of this. And another thing: we don't have enough white silk lace or ordinary lace, so some more needs to be bought, because Mr Bykov says he doesn't want his wife going around like a cook, and I must be sure to 'put all the landowners' wives' noses out of joint'. That's what he himself says. So, Makar Alexeyevich, take yourself off, please, to Mme Chiffon on Gorokhovaya and ask her firstly to send some seamstresses to us, and secondly to take the trouble to come herself as well. I'm ill today. Our new apartment's so cold, and in dreadful disorder. Mr Bykov's auntie can hardly breathe, she's so old. I'm afraid she might die before our departure, but Mr Bykov says it's alright, she'll recover. The house is in dreadful disorder. Mr Bykov isn't living with us, so all the servants run off God knows where. There are times when Fedora's serving us by herself; while Mr Bykov's valet, who looks after everything, is missing, no one knows where, for the third day now. Mr Bykov drops in every morning, keeps getting angry, and yesterday hit the house steward, which caused him some unpleasantness with the police... There's been nobody to send to you with letters. I'm writing by the city post. Yes! I almost forgot the most important thing. Tell Mme Chiffon to be sure to change the white silk lace in accordance with yesterday's sample, and to call on me herself to show me the new selection. And tell her as well that I've changed my mind about the canezou; that it should be crocheted. And another thing: the letters for the monograms on the handkerchiefs should be embroidered in chain-stitch; do you hear? In chain-stitch, not satin-stitch. Mind you don't forget, in chain-stitch! There's something else I almost forgot! For God's sake tell her that the leaves on the pelerine should be in raised stitching, the tendrils and thorns should be in *cordonnet*, and then the collar should be trimmed with lace or a wide falbala. Please tell her, Makar Alexeyevich.

Your

V. D.

PS I feel so guilty that I keep on troubling you with my errands. This is the third day you've spent the whole morning running around. But what's to be done? There's no order at home here, and I'm unwell myself. So don't be annoyed with me, Makar Alexeyevich. Such anguish! Ah, what's going to happen, my friend, my dear, my kind Makar Alexeyevich! I'm afraid even to take a look into my future. I have a constant premonition of something, and it's as if I'm living in some sort of fog.

PS For God's sake, my friend, don't forget anything of what I've just been telling you. I keep worrying in case you make some mistake. And remember, chain-stitch, not satin-stitch.

V. D.

27TH SEPTEMBER

Madam, Varvara Alexeyevna!
I've carried out all your errands assiduously. Mme Chiffon says she was herself already thinking of doing the trimming in chain-stitch; that it's more respectable or something, I don't know, I didn't grasp it very well. And another thing, you wrote about a falbala, well she said something about a falbala too, only I've forgotten, my dear, what she said about a falbala. I only remember she said a great deal; such an awful woman! Now what was it? Well, she'll tell you everything herself. I'm completely fagged out, my dear. I didn't go to work today either. Only you've no reason to despair, my dear. For your peace of mind I'm prepared to run around all the shops. You write that you're afraid to take a look into the future. But after all, by seven o'clock today you'll know everything. Mme Chiffon will come and see you herself. So don't you despair; have hope, my dear; and maybe everything will turn out for the best – there. So yes, that damned falbala, I keep – oh, I'm fed up with that falbala, the falbala! I'd pop in to see you, little angel, I'd pop in, I'd definitely pop in; as it is I've walked up to the gates of your house a couple of times. Only it's Bykov, that is, I mean, Mr Bykov is always so angry, so that it's not quite… Well, so what!

Makar Devushkin

Dear Sir, Makar Alexeyevich!
For God's sake, run to the jeweller straight away. Tell him there's no need to make the pearl and emerald earrings. Mr Bykov says it's too grand, that it's exorbitant. He's angry; he says he's spending a fortune as it is and that we're robbing him, and yesterday he said that if he'd had the least inkling beforehand of such expenses, he wouldn't have got involved. He says that just as soon as we're wed, we'll be leaving straight away, that there'll be no guests, and that I shouldn't entertain hopes of spinning and twirling, that party-time is still a long way off. That's the way he talks! And God knows if I need all this! Mr Bykov has ordered everything himself. I don't dare even to answer him anything: he's so hot-tempered. What will become of me?

V. D.

Sweetheart, Varvara Alexeyevna!
I – that is the jeweller says – alright; but I wanted to say of myself first that I've fallen ill and can't get out of bed. Right now, when a busy, vital time's arrived, that's when I get an attack of the chills, the devil take them! I also inform you that on top of all my misfortunes, His Excellency has been good enough to be strict as well, and got very angry with Yemelyan Ivanovich, and shouted, and towards the end was completely worn out, the poor man. So here I am informing you about everything. And I wanted to write you something else too, only I'm afraid of troubling you. After all, my dear, I'm a stupid, simple man, I write anything that comes into my head, so perhaps there's something you might even – well, so what!
   Your

Makar Devushkin

Varvara Alexeyevna, my dear!

I saw Fedora today, sweetheart. She says that tomorrow you'll already be wed, and you'll be going the day after tomorrow, and that Mr Bykov is already hiring the horses. I've already informed you regarding His Excellency, my dear. And another thing: I've checked the bills from the shop on Gorokhovaya; everything's correct, only very expensive. Only why is it that Mr Bykov gets angry with you? Well, be happy, my dear! I'm glad; yes, I'll be glad if you're happy. I'd come to the church, my dear, but I can't, I've got lumbago. So I'm still talking about letters: I mean, who will deliver them to us now, my dear? Yes! You were charitable to Fedora, my dear! It was a good deed you did, my friend; it was a very good thing you did. A good deed! And for every good deed the Lord will bless you. Good deeds don't go unrewarded, and virtue will always be crowned with the crown of God's justice, sooner or later. My dear! I'd like to write you a lot, so that every hour, every minute I'd keep on writing, I'd keep on writing! I still have one of your books, *The Tales of Belkin*, but, you know, my dear, don't you take it away from me, give it to me, sweetheart. It's not because I want to read it so very much. But you know yourself, my dear, winter's coming; the evenings will be long; it'll be sad, then would be the time for a read. I'll move from my apartment to your old one, my dear, and I'll rent from Fedora. I'll not part for anything now from that honest woman; what's more, she's so hard-working. I had a good look at your empty apartment yesterday. As your tambour was, and on it your sewing, so it's remained there, untouched: it's in the corner. I examined your embroidery. Some pieces still remain here. You were just beginning to wind thread onto one of my letters. In a drawer I found a sheet of paper, and on the paper was written: "Dear Sir, Makar Alexeyevich, I make haste' – and that was all. Someone evidently interrupted you at the most interesting place. In the corner behind the little screens stands your bed… Sweetheart!!! Well, goodbye, goodbye; for God's sake let me have some reply to this letter quickly.

Makar Devushkin

My priceless friend, Makar Alexeyevich!

All is done! My lot has been cast, what it will be, I don't know, but I submit to the will of the Lord. We're leaving tomorrow. I'm bidding you farewell for the last time, my priceless friend, my benefactor, my dear! Don't grieve over me, live happily, remember me, and may God's blessing be upon you! I shall remember you often in my thoughts and in my prayers. So this time has come to an end! I shall carry little of comfort into my new life from memories of the past; all the more dear will be the memory of you, all the more dear will you be to my heart. You are my only friend; just you alone loved me here. For I saw everything, you know, I knew how you loved me! You were happy with one smile from me, with one line of my writing. Now you'll have to try to get along without me! How will you stay here by yourself? Who here will look after you, my good, my priceless, my only friend! I'm leaving you the book, the tambour, the letter I started; whenever you look at these lines I began, read on in your thoughts everything you'd like to hear or read from me, everything I might have written you; and what might I have written now! Think of your poor Varenka, who loved you so much. All your letters are still in the top drawer of Fedora's chest of drawers. You write that you're ill, but Mr Bykov isn't letting me go out anywhere today. I shall write to you, my friend, I promise, but then God alone knows what might happen. And so now we'll say farewell forever, my friend, sweetheart, my dear, forever!… Oh, how I'd like to hold you now! Farewell, my friend, farewell, farewell. Live happily; keep well. My prayer will always be for you. Oh, how sad I am, how crushed my whole spirit. Mr Bykov is calling me. Your eternally loving

V.

PS My soul is so full, so full now of tears…
Tears are constricting me, tearing me apart. Farewell.
God! What sadness!
Remember, remember your poor Varenka!

My dear, Varenka, sweetheart, my priceless one! You're being carried off, you're going! It'd be better now if they tore the heart from my breast, than you from me! How can you? So you're crying, but you're going? I've just now received the letter from you all spotted with tears. That means you don't want to go; that means you're being carried off forcibly, that means you feel sorry for me, that means you love me! But I don't understand, who will you be with now? Your little heart will be sad, sick and cold there. Anguish will gnaw at it, sadness will tear it in two. You'll die there, they'll lay you in the cold earth there; there'll be nobody even to cry over you there! Mr Bykov will be hunting hares all the time… Ah, my dear, my dear! What is it you've resolved upon, how could you resolve upon such a step? What have you done, what have you done, what have you done to yourself? I mean, you'll be driven to your grave there; they'll wear you out there, my little angel. I mean, you're delicate as a feather, my dear. And where was I? Why was I just staring like an idiot? I can see the child's being silly, the little child's just got a headache. Instead of just simply – but oh no, I'm a complete idiot, and I don't think anything, and I don't see anything, as if I'm right and as if it's none of my business; and on top of that I went running around about a falbala!… No, Varenka, I'll get up; perhaps I'll be better by tomorrow, and then I'll get up!… I'll throw myself under the wheels, my dear; I won't let you go away! No, really, what is all this? By what rights is all this being done? I'll go away with you; I'll run after your carriage, if you won't take me, I'll run for all I'm worth until I drop dead. Only do you know what it's like there, where it is you're going, my dear? Perhaps you don't know, so then ask me! There's the steppe there, my dear, there's the steppe, the bare steppe; bare as the palm of my hand! There's peasants there, unfeeling women and uneducated men, there's drunkards. The leaves have fallen from the trees there now, it's raining there, it's cold – and you're going there! Well, Mr Bykov has something to do there: he'll be with the hares there; but what about you? You want to be a landowner's wife, my dear? But my little cherub, you just take a look at yourself, do you look like a landowner's wife?… How can it possibly be, Varenka? Who will I write letters to, my dear? Yes! You just take into consideration, my dear – 'who will he write letters to?' Who will I call 'my dear'; who will I call by such a nice name? Where am I to find you later on, my little angel? I'll die, Varenka, I'm sure to die; my heart won't survive such a misfortune! I loved you like the Lord's light, like my own daughter, I loved everything about you, my dear, my love! And I myself lived for just you alone! I worked, and I wrote documents, and went about, and went for walks, and transferred my observations onto paper in the form of letters to a friend, all because of the fact that you, my dear, lived here, opposite, nearby. Perhaps you didn't even know it, but it was all exactly like that! Just listen, my dear, you judge, sweetheart, how can it possibly be that you've left us? My dear, you mustn't go, you know, it's not possible; there's simply definitely no possibility at all! I mean, it's raining, and you're weak, you'll catch cold. Your carriage will get wet; it's sure to get wet. As soon as you leave the city gate, it'll break down too; it'll break down on purpose. Here in St Petersburg they make carriages really badly, you know! I know all those coach-builders too; they only want to make something fashionable, some smart toy, but they don't make them sturdy, I swear they don't! I'll throw myself on my knees before Mr Bykov, my dear; I'll make him see, I'll make him see everything! And you make him see too, my dear; reason with him and make him see! Tell him you're staying, that you can't leave!... Ah, why is it he didn't marry the merchant's widow in Moscow? He should've married her there! The merchant's widow would be better, she'd suit him much better; and I know why! And I'd keep you here with me. What is he to you, my dear, this Bykov? How has he suddenly made himself dear to you? Perhaps it's because he keeps buying you falbalas, perhaps that's why it is? But I mean, what's a falbala? Why a falbala? After all, my dear, it's nonsense! We're talking about a human life here, my dear, whereas a falbala is, you know, just cloth; a falbala, my dear – it's just a bit of cloth. As soon as I get my salary, I'll buy you loads of falbalas myself; I'll buy you loads of them, my dear; there's even this little shop I know; just let me wait for my salary. Varenka, my little cherub! Oh God, God! So you're definitely leaving for the steppe with Mr Bykov, leaving and not coming back! Ah, my dear!... No, you write some more to me, write me another nice letter about everything, and when you leave, write me a letter from there as well. Otherwise, my heavenly angel, this will be the last letter, you know; but I mean it can't possibly be the case that this letter should be the last. I mean, how could it be, so suddenly, absolutely, definitely the last? But no, I'll write, and you write too... Because my style's taking shape now too... Ah my dear, what about style! I mean, I don't even know now what it is I'm writing, I don't know at all, I don't know anything, and I'm not rereading and I'm not correcting the style, but I'm writing for the sake of writing, just for the sake of writing some more to you... Sweetheart, my love, my dear!

1. The epigraph is a slightly inaccurate quotation from Odoevsky's story *The Living Dead Man* (1844).

2. Baron Brambeus was one of the literary pseudonyms of Osip Senkovsky, editor of the popular journal *The Library for Reading*, and a favourite of less sophisticated readers.

3. The names of the two servants are borrowed from the protagonists of the French novel *The Letters of Two Lovers Living in Lyons* (1783) by Nicolas-Germain Léonard, published in Russian translation in 1804 and 1816.

4. Gostiny Dvor is the arcaded trading area on Nevsky Avenue.

5. The first two extracts from Ratazyayev's writing are pastiches of popular styles, but the third is specifically modelled on Nikolai Gogol's *The Squabble, or The Tale of How Ivan Ivanovich Fell Out with Ivan Nikiforovich* (1835).

6. Paul de Kock, a prolific French novelist, was considered by conservative critics to be coarse and risqué.

7. *The Northern Bee* was a notoriously conservative newspaper with an unsophisticated readership.

BIOGRAPHICAL NOTE

Fyodor Mikhailovich Dostoevsky (1821–1881) was born in Moscow. After the death of his mother in 1837, he was sent to the St Petersburg Engineering Academy, where he studied for five years and eventually graduated as an engineer. In 1844, however, Dostoevsky gave up engineering to write. His translation of Balzac's *Eugénie Grandet* came out in 1844, and his first novel, *Poor People*, was published in 1846. During this time Dostoevsky also became interested in Utopian Socialism – a political affiliation which would lead to his deportation, in 1850, to Siberia. He was imprisoned for four years in a penal settlement, and served for four more thereafter as a soldier in Semipalatinsk. The experience changed his life and writing: whilst in prison he became a member of the Russian Orthodox Church, a monarchist, and upon his return to Moscow, he wrote about his experience as a prisoner in *Notes from the House of the Dead* (1862).

In 1862, Dostoevsky travelled around Europe for the first time, an experience which also marked his writing. He was a great admirer of the English novel, in particular the works of Charles Dickens, but he disliked Europe. London, above all, was Dostoevsky's 'Baal', the centre of world capitalism, and he used the Crystal Palace as a symbol of the corrupting influence of modernity in *Notes from Underground* (1864). Upon his return to Russia, Dostoevsky wrote some of his best novels, including *Crime and Punishment* (1866), *The Idiot* (1868) and *The Brothers Karamazov* (1880) which he completed just before his death.

Having been largely ignored by English language readers in the nineteenth century, Dostoevsky is now considered to be the most popular and influential Russian author read in the twentieth and twenty-first centuries. The penetrating psychological nature of Dostoevsky's novels, his obsessive grappling with conscience, guilt and God, as well as the brilliance of his characterisation and plots, continue to inspire new generations of readers, writers and thinkers. Dostoevsky's novels are undisputed masterpieces.

Hugh Aplin studied Russian at the University of East Anglia and Voronezh State University, and worked at the Universities of Leeds and St Andrews before taking up his current post as Head of Russian at Westminster School, London.

HESPERUS PRESS – 100 PAGES

Hesperus Press, as suggested by the Latin motto, is committed to bringing near what is far – far both in space and time. Works written by the greatest authors, and unjustly neglected or simply little known in the English-speaking world, are made accessible through new translations and a completely fresh editorial approach. Through these short classic works, each little more than 100 pages in length, the reader will be introduced to the greatest writers from all times and all cultures.

For more information on Hesperus Press, please visit our website:
www.hesperuspress.com

To place an order, please contact:
Grantham Book Services
Isaac Newton Way
Alma Park Industrial Estate
Grantham
Lincolnshire NG31 9SD
Tel: +44 (0) 1476 541080
Fax: +44 (0) 1476 541061
Email: orders@gbs.tbs-ltd.co.uk

SELECTED TITLES FROM HESPERUS PRESS

Gustave Flaubert *Memoirs of a Madman*
Alexander Pope *Scriblerus*
Ugo Foscolo *Last Letters of Jacopo Ortis*
Anton Chekhov *The Story of a Nobody*
Joseph von Eichendorff *Life of a Good-for-nothing*
Mark Twain *The Diary of Adam and Eve*
Giovanni Boccaccio *Life of Dante*
Victor Hugo *The Last Day of a Condemned Man*
Joseph Conrad *Heart of Darkness*
Edgar Allan Poe *Eureka*
Emile Zola *For a Night of Love*
Daniel Defoe *The King of Pirates*
Giacomo Leopardi *Thoughts*
Nikolai Gogol *The Squabble*
Franz Kafka *Metamorphosis*
Herman Melville *The Enchanted Isles*
Leonardo da Vinci *Prophecies*
Charles Baudelaire *On Wine and Hashish*
William Makepeace Thackeray *Rebecca and Rowena*
Wilkie Collins *Who Killed Zebedee?*
Théophile Gautier *The Jinx*
Charles Dickens *The Haunted House*
Luigi Pirandello *Loveless Love*
E.T.A. Hoffmann *Mademoiselle de Scudéri*
Henry James *In the Cage*
Francis Petrarch *My Secret Book*
André Gide *Theseus*
D.H. Lawrence *The Fox*
Percy Bysshe Shelley *Zastrozzi*